D.J. saw a little girl about five years old standing on
top of a picnic table. She was shrieking hysterically,
an empty ice cream cone gripped in both hands.
The scoop of ice cream lay on the attached redwood bench. A cinnamon-colored young bear was
enthusiastically licking the ice cream.

D.J. raced across the grass. He grabbed the broken
chain and pulled the cub firmly away from the last
signs of the ice cream. Koko bounced playfully
against D.J.'s legs, smearing ice cream on his clean
pants.

"Oh, Koko! Look what you've done!"

LEE RODDY is a best-selling author of more than 50 books. He lives in the Sierra Nevada Mountains of California and devotes his time to writing books and public speaking. He is a co-writer of the book which became the TV series, "The Life and Times of Grizzly Adams."

Born on an Illinois farm and reared on a California ranch, Lee Roddy grew up around hunters and trail hounds. As a boy, he began writing animal stories. He spent lots of time reading about dogs, horses, and other animals. These stories shaped his thinking and values before he went to Hollywood to write professionally. His Christian commitment later turned his writing talents to books like this one.

This is the second book in the D.J. Dillon Adventure Series.

The Bear Cub Disaster

LEE RODDY

VICTOR BOOKS
A DIVISION OF SCRIPTURE PRESS PUBLICATIONS INC.
USA CANADA ENGLAND

THE D.J. DILLON
ADVENTURE SERIES

THE HAIR-PULLING BEAR DOG
THE BEAR CUB DISASTER
DOOGER, THE GRASSHOPPER HOUND
THE GHOST DOG OF STONEY RIDGE
MAD DOG OF LOBO MOUNTAIN
THE LEGEND OF THE WHITE RACCOON
THE MYSTERY OF THE BLACK HOLE MINE
GHOST OF THE MOANING MANSION
THE SECRET OF MAD RIVER
ESCAPE DOWN THE RAGING RAPIDS

Most Scripture quotations in the book are from the *New American Standard Bible,*
© the Lockman Foundation, 1960, 1962, 1963, 1968, 1971, 1972, 1973, 1975, 1977. Other quotations are from the *King James Version.*

 7 8 9 10 11 12 13 14 15 16 Printing/Year 00 99 98 97 96

Library of Congress Catalog Card Number: 84-52030
ISBN: 1-56476-503-2

CONTENTS

To my brothers
Joe, Jim, and Jack Roddy
who let me practice
telling stories to them
while we were growing up

Chapter One

CAPTURE OF A WILD BEAR CUB

Thirteen-year-old D.J. Dillon peered anxiously through the pickup's dusty windshield. Slowly the truck growled out of Devil's Slide Canyon, away from Mad River. Paul Stagg, a giant of a man, steered the borrowed truck along a logging road in California's high Sierra Nevada Mountains. On the floorboards, Hero, D.J's little hair-pulling bear dog,* slept with his muzzle across the boy's dusty, cork-soled boots.

D.J. kept his blue eyes on the beautiful green forest of conifers* standing tall in the summer sun. He asked, "You think there's a chance?"

Paul Stagg chuckled. It was a low, rumbling sound that bubbled up from his big chest. "Never can tell, D.J., though I didn't see anything like a bear cub yesterday. But we'll stop in a minute and take a look."

*You can find an explanation of the starred words under "Life in Stoney Ridge" on pages 128-130.

The boy twisted in the seat to look out the back window. Several trail hounds rested in their box in the back of the pickup. The boy raised his right hand and brushed the pale yellowish hair back from his eyes. He could see a culvert trap secured on the trailer which bounced behind the pickup. Both iron-barred doors were down and locked on the trap.

Through the nearest barred door, the boy saw the outlaw bear, Ol' Satchel Foot, riding unharmed in the trap. In an exciting adventure, Ol' Satchel Foot had been captured alive. Now his infected jaw could be treated before he was trucked higher into the mountains and released. Twelve-year-old Kathy Stagg, Paul's daughter, would be very happy about that.

Suddenly, Paul Stagg raised one huge hand and pointed. "That's where it happened."

"I see her!" D.J. exclaimed, leaning forward. "And look over there! She *did* have a cub! Look at him run for that tree!"

The cub wasn't much bigger than a house cat. He was a kind of cinnamon color like his mother who lay dead under a sugar pine.* The cub scooted up the tree's rough trunk and disappeared into the branches.

"He'll starve to death!" D.J. exclaimed. "He'll die unless we capture him and take him home so I can raise him!"

"D.J., you're asking for more problems than any boy should have if you take a wild creature out of its native place."

"But *you* once had a cub!"

"That's why I'm telling you it's going to give you troubles!"

"But we can't just let him die! Please? Let's capture him!"

Paul pushed up his rolled-brim cowboy hat with a strong forefinger. "Well, considering what you've been through, D.J., I guess you're entitled to do that."

In a few minutes, the man and the boy had alighted from the pickup truck and quieted the hounds. The dogs had smelled the dead mother bear which Tinsley Abst and his son had been forced to shoot the day before. Hero, the scruffy little hair-pulling dog, sniffed once at the big bear's carcass and immediately followed the cub's scent to the tree. The dog jumped up on the tree, scratching and trying to climb it.

D.J. said, "No, Zero! I mean—Hero!" The mixture of hound, Airedale, and Australian shepherd had earned a name change after some encounters with bears that had nearly cost the little dog his life. Now the mutt tucked his stub of a tail between his hind legs and looked uncertainly at the boy. D.J. bent and gave the dog a quick pat. "I know you did a good thing in treeing that little fellow, Hero, but you'll scare him if you bark like that. Now, lie down and stay out of the way while Paul and I figure out how to get that cub down."

The big man was a volunteer lay preacher who had recently come to pastor the community church at Stoney Ridge. Paul stood nearly seven feet tall with his peaked cowboy hat and high-heeled boots. He had already hooked some dog chains together and was now making a loop in the end of the first chain. "D.J., this worked for me years ago when I caught my cub, so it should work again. You climb up there in that ponderosa tree* closest to the sugar pine where the cub is. Find a long pointed stick— one with a little Y in it—and take it up with you."

"Then what?"

"I'll tell you that when you get up alongside that cub. Meanwhile, I'll dig out an extra tin coat and an old leather jacket I've got in the pickup." A tin coat was made of very sturdy material so loggers couldn't easily tear it while working in the timber.

D.J. was tall for his age, very fair, and quite strong. He scampered up the tree, taking care to keep the chains from snagging on limbs. When he was alongside the cub, he spoke quietly to him. "I know you're scared and your mama's dead. But we're here to help you. Just take it easy and you'll soon have something to eat."

Paul's big booming voice came up from the ground. "You ready, D.J.?"

"Ready!"

"OK, hang on tight with one hand so you don't fall. Take the stick and put it in the loop of chain I made. When you're ready, ease the stick out toward the cub. Try to drop the loop over his head."

It sounded easy enough to the boy, but the little bear bit the Y-stick and swatted the chain away with a forepaw. D.J. tried again.

"Now look, little cub, I'm trying to help you! So don't make it hard for me!"

The boy again eased the stick forward with the chain on the end. The cinnamon-colored cub swung his forepaw again. The chain fell hard against D.J.'s tin pants.

The boy reset the stick's Y into the loop of chain

and eased it out again. This time, he held it above
the cub's head and out of reach. The bear's bright
eyes watched as the loop and stick slowly descend-
ed. Suddenly, the bear's left forepaw struck. The
stick was caught and bent down sharply. The chain
slid heavily down, hitting on the cub's head. For a
second, the chain caught on the bear's right ear.
The cub tried to shake it off, but the chain settled
like a bright silver necklace around the cub's neck.

"Gotcha!" D.J. cried, pulling slack out of the
chain so the cub couldn't throw it off, but not so
tight the bear would choke. The boy raised his
voice. "I got him, Paul! Now what?"

"Slowly tighten the chain loop about his neck,
then pull steadily but carefully until the cub lets go
his hold."

D.J. obeyed, fighting some concern that the cub
would be hurt. But the 15-pound bear was no match
for the heavier boy. In a moment, the little forepaws
were pulled free. As the boy continued to pull, the
cub's hind paws were also pulled free of the limb.

"He's free!"

"Good!" Paul Stagg's voice boomed through the
dense green pine needles. "Now lower him down
to me! Keep him steady, but lower him fast so we
don't hurt him."

The boy leaned his shoulder against the tree
trunk so he could use both hands. The cub
squealed as he was lowered through the limbs,
pulled free as he tried to hang on, and finally
cleared the bottom limbs.

"Can you reach him, Paul?"

"One more second! There! OK, I've got my tin

coat around him! Get down here as fast as you can and help me get the other coat around him before he tears this one up and me with it!"

The boy tossed the chain away from him so it wouldn't fall on the man. It fell heavily to the brown pine needles under the trees. Then D.J. scrambled backward down the tree. When he was about six feet up, he pushed himself out and away. He fell to his knees, jumped up, and grabbed the leather coat which he threw over the cub's snapping mouth.

"Whew!" Paul said, helping make the second coat into a tighter wrap. "I was having a tough time letting go of that little bear!"

"Is he hurt? Will he smother?"

"No. He can breath through that coat while I put a little rawhide wrap around his jaws so he can't bite us. Right now, he's just real scared, I reckon. Well, he can't tear up both those coats before we get him home. Here, let's lift him into the front seat between us and then head for your place. I got a hunch your father's not going to take kindly to this new pet!"

The big lay preacher was right. D.J. chained the hounds and Hero at the creek below the house because Paul Stagg couldn't leave the outlaw bear and the cage. D.J. waded the creek without removing his boots, holding the wrapped cub in both coats. The boy hurried up the dusty, rutted, and unpaved road to the tiny little house where he lived with his father and grandfather.

Grandpa Dillon was rocking in his cane-bottom chair on the front porch, his Irish shillelagh* resting across his lap. The old man raised his pale-blue eyes and called, "What's that there thing you're a'holding, D.J.?"

"You'd never guess, Grandpa!"

The old man snorted and adjusted the bifocals on his nose. "Trouble, more'n likely." He raised his voice and turned to call inside the house. "D.J.'s back!"

The boy's father appeared at the screen door. Sam Dillon was a short, powerfully built man with a darkly tanned face from working as a choke-setter* in the timber.

"Dad, guess what? I found my little hair-pulling bear dog alive! And we also caught Ol' Satchel Foot alive! Hero helped me save Nails Abst from getting hurt or killed, and then Paul Stagg and I found this bear cub, and I'd like to—"

"Bear cub!" Dad's words exploded like his long-barreled Krag rifle. "You're bringing a wild critter like that into this house?"

The boy removed the leather jacket from the cub's head and slipped Hero's chain over the animal's head. "Ah, Dad, he's not any bigger than a cat, and he can't hurt me! Could I keep him, huh, please? If I don't, he'll starve, because that professional bear hunter and his son killed the mother bear. Please, Dad!"

Sam Dillon's face clouded up with black anger, but before he could yell as D.J. knew he was about to do, Grandpa spoke quietly.

"If you'd got killed out there chasing that outlaw bear, D.J., your father and I would have given anything to have you back safe and sound. Isn't that right, Sam?"

Since D.J.'s mother had been killed in an auto accident, the two men argued all the time. But Grandpa had recently given his life to the Lord, and he'd not been arguing with his son Sam, D.J.'s father.

D.J. waited anxiously, his blue eyes pleading with his strong-willed father. Dad glared at Grandpa for a long time before finally answering.

"D.J., I'm dead set against it because I'm sure we're heading for trouble, but, well—"

"Thanks, Dad! Hey! Grandpa! Look! I've got both a dog and a bear cub! Now if I only had some boy who could be my best friend!"

Grandpa cackled like a Rhode Island Red hen. "D.J., you sure got a powerful lot of wants for one boy! Well, now, if you're going to have a bear cub for a pet, we'd best name him."

"You think of a name while I go back and get the hounds, Grandpa."

When the boy had returned from the creek and chained the hounds under the L-shaped front porch, Grandpa had decided.

"Named him 'Teddy,' 'cause he's the color of that teddy bear you used to have, D.J."

Before the boy could answer, Dad exploded. "*Teddy?* What kind of a name is *that* for a real bear? Besides, D.J.'s teddy bear was more brown or reddish brown; cocoa-colored! But look how tough this little cub already is! He's tearing up those coats, and him with his mouth tied shut! So I say his name's Tuffy—not Teddy!"

Grandpa clicked his false teeth. "It's Teddy! Not—"

He broke off suddenly and glanced skyward.

"Whoops! I plumb forgot! You all call him anything you want, and I'll go along with you."

D.J. looked at Grandpa in surprise, then understood. The old man was trying to follow peaceful paths instead of arguing about everything as he always had before.

Dad's black temper was close to the surface again, D.J. saw. Dad goaded his father. "You giving up without an argument?"

Grandpa looked at his son. "I'm a'going to live like a changed man, the good Lord helping. You'll get nary a contrary word out of me over this!"

D.J. spoke up before his dad could say anything more. "I think I'll just call him cocoa because of his color. Only I'll spell it K-O-K-O."

Dad said, "That cub's more cinnamon-colored than cocoa-colored."

D.J. was surprised to hear Grandpa say, "Does that make much difference, Sam? Why can't the boy call the bear anything he wants, regardless of its color?"

Dad shrugged. "Yeah, why not? Koko's OK, I guess."

"Fine with me too," Grandpa said.

For the first time D.J. could remember, he gave something a name which both his father and grandfather agreed to recognize. The boy fed the cub and was surprised to find that, little as he was, the bear ate almost anything and asked for more.

In a few days, the cub had learned to come to a tug of a dog chain attached to a thick leather collar Grandpa had made from a piece of old harness. D.J. was pleased because the cub learned to lead

more quickly than a dog. In a week, D.J. was ready
to show off his pet in town. As Grandpa said, "That
bear was born tame! Why, you'd think he was a city
bear instead of being born wild!"

D.J. rode into town with his father. Sam Dillon
parked his old pickup truck at the high curb in
front of the town's only mercantile store. Dad went
inside to buy some groceries. D.J. snapped the
chain onto the cub's collar and led him slowly
down the sidewalk.

Everybody stared. Two cars almost collided in
the street as the drivers turned to look at the bear.
D.J. felt good. As he passed an alley, he heard
someone yell, "You leave me alone!"

D.J. stopped and looked into the alley. He recognized 14-year-old Nails Abst, but not the smaller
boy. The bigger kid held the front of the other boy's
shirt so he was almost lifted off the ground. Nails
kicked at a loaf of bread that the smaller boy had
obviously dropped. But the smaller boy was strug-
gling hard against the town bully's grip.

D.J. was surprised to hear himself yell, "Hey,
Nails! Let him go!" Instantly, D.J. wished he hadn't
done that.

Chapter Two

THE ICE CREAM-EATING BEAR

Nails Abst spun to look at D.J. The older boy reminded D.J. of a sourpuss that had just swallowed a gallon of vinegar. His face looked as though a whole herd of horses had run over it. That was from fighting almost every kid in town. D.J. was almost as tall as Nails, but he was slender as a ski pole and weighed less than the older boy. Nails, son of professional bear hunter Tinsley Abst, let go of the strange boy's shirt and started for D.J.

"Well, now!" Nails said, clenching his strong fists and forcing muscles to show from his short-sleeved shirt. "If it isn't D.J. Dillon!"

"Hi, Nails." D.J. said it quietly, hoping to keep out of trouble. The fact that he had saved Nails' life a few days earlier when the outlaw bear had trapped them on a hunting trip wouldn't count for much now, D.J. knew. The older boy didn't like people telling him what to do.

D.J. saw the skinny kid in the alley pick up his loaf of bread and start down the alley the other way. Then the kid stopped and looked back. He used his right forefinger to push his eyeglasses higher up on his nose. The glasses were so thick they almost looked like the bottom of a soda-pop bottle.

Suddenly, Nails pointed at the cub. "What's that?"

"My new bear cub."

"Where'd you get him?"

"Remember that sow you and your father shot when you were chasing Ol' Satchel Foot?"

"Had to kill her! Our hounds ran across her accidentlylike, and she was eating up our dogs!"

"Well, no matter. She's dead, and I found this cub by her carcass when we came out with Ol' Satchel Foot in the cage trap."

"Yeah?" Nails bent and reached for the cub. The bear suddenly lifted his forepaw and swiped at the older boy. He jerked his hand back. "Hey! He tried to hurt me! I'll fix him!"

Nails picked up a two-foot-long tree limb and violently swung it down toward the cub. Instinctively, D.J. threw up his hand and blocked the blow. The limb spun out of Nails' hand and struck him across the nose before clattering to the ground. "Ouch! Ow! Ow! You did that on purpose!" Nails' thick neck turned red and his face blackened like a storm cloud. "Now you've done it, D.J. Dillon! I'm going to fix you good; then I'm going to take that cub!"

D.J. blurted, "Take my cub?"

"It's not your cub! I killed the mother and so the cub's rightfully mine! Now hand it over!"

D.J. backed up, pulling the cub's chain to bring

the animal in back of him. Out of the corner of his eye, D.J. saw the new kid run up behind Nails.

"Hey!" the new kid yelled. "You leave him alone!"

Nails turned around and laughed. "Why, you little half-pint of nothing, I'll teach you both a lesson!"

A man's voice snapped, "Nails! Quit fooling around and get in this car!"

All three boys turned toward the curb. None had seen an old black pickup pull to the high sidewalk. D.J. recognized Tinsley Abst, Nails' father. He and Nails had recently come to Stoney Ridge to try for the bounty on Ol' Satchel Foot. But the hunter had withdrawn any claim to the reward after D.J. and his little dog had saved Nails' life.

Nails raised his voice. "Yeah, Pa! I'm a'coming!" Nails lowered his voice. "I know where to find you, D.J.! I'll be back after my bear. As for you, kid— what's your name?"

"Alfred." The newcomer said it quietly, looking at the bigger boy out of thick glasses. He was skinny as an old horse with ribs that showed even through his patched blue work-shirt that once had been a man's.

Nails growled, "Well, Alfred, I hope you slept good last night, 'cause you're not ever going to rest easy, knowing I'm going to whop you good every time I see you the rest of your life."

Alfred exclaimed, "I'm not afraid of you!"

Nails sneered. "Shows how dumb you are, kid! Well, D.J., take good care of my bear until I get back."

D.J. swallowed hard and watched the bigger kid get into the black pickup and ride away with his father.

"Thanks," Alfred said. "He wanted my money, but my folks don't have a lot, so I wouldn't give it up." He reached into his pocket and pulled out four pennies.

D.J. frowned. "That's what you were scuffling about?"

"Not the four cents; the principle. That's what my folks always say. I've got more money of my own."

Suddenly, D.J. laughed right out loud. "Alfred, I like you! My name's D.J. Dillon, and this here's Koko."

"I'm Alfred Milford. Can I pet your bear?"

"Don't really know. Never had him out in public before. But if you reach down slow and easy, maybe he'll let you touch him."

Alfred bent slowly and reached the back of his hand toward the cub. The bear sniffed it and licked it. Both boys laughed.

"Must smell the bread on it," Alfred said. "Hey, I got enough money for an ice cream. Let's get it in a dish so you and I can both have some, and we'll let the cub lick the plate."

Stoney Ridge had one small store that was a combination drugstore, soda fountain, and magazine rack. The two boys walked in to the smell of medicines and dust. The place was old and cramped. The owner, Mr. Gurney, looked up from behind the counter. He tipped his head down to look over his half-glasses. "Now, boys, you're right welcome, but you'll have to park your horse outside." He laughed at his own joke, which was echoed by a girl's light laughter. D.J. glanced over to the greeting card section where Kathy Stagg was looking at a card. She hurried up to D.J., her reddish-colored hair flying out behind her.

"Oh, D.J.! I've been wanting to tell you how much I appreciated you helping capture that sick outlaw bear alive! The vet says Ol' Satchel Foot's responding to antibiotics* real well. Soon he'll be healthy enough to be released up in the high country."

D.J. didn't know what to say. He managed to introduce Alfred and Paul Stagg's daughter. They exchanged "hi's" and then Kathy left. She paused at the door, glanced at the cub, and raised her voice to D.J. "You're surely not thinking of keeping that cub in captivity, are you?"

D.J. didn't want another argument with her. Since they'd first met a few weeks ago, she didn't hesitate to tell him what she didn't like about what he was doing. But Priscilla Higgins, a nine-year-old girl who went to D.J.'s school, had said Kathy thought D.J. was cute. Every time he thought of that, he felt his neck get hot.

He answered Kathy's question. "I just saved that cub's life; your father and me, anyway." D.J. took a red-topped plastic stool at the ice cream counter and motioned for Alfred to do the same.

Kathy's snapping blue eyes seemed to flame. "Well," she said, "the sooner you turn him loose in the mountains, the better." She closed the door and hurried down the street.

Alfred said, "She's kind of snippy and sassy, isn't she?"

"Some," D.J. admitted. "My dad calls her 'spunky.' Her father—Paul Stagg, he's a lay preacher for our church—and I caught an outlaw bear in a special trap. We were coming out of the mountains when we found that cub." D.J. turned to look out the front door. A stray dog ran up to the cub as if Koko were another dog. The cub swatted at the dog which yelped and ran away, tail between its legs.

Mr. Gurney put a small dish of strawberry ice cream before the boys. "Two spoons, I suppose? Or will you eat it with your fingers?" He laughed at his own joke. "Say, D.J., the newspaper was full of what you and the lay preacher did a week or so ago. What're you going to do with that cub?"

"Don't really know, Mr. Gurney. I couldn't let him starve."

"You could give him away."

"Who'd want him?"

"Oh, I don't know. Tinsley Abst hunts bears for money. Maybe he'd know what to do."

D.J. shook his head. "His son'd only hurt the cub. Nails already showed that when me 'n Alfred met."

"Alfred, is it? You must be John Milford's son. Met your father last week when he came in for some toothache medication. No strangers in Stoney Ridge, you know—anyway, not for long. You really like ice cream, don't you, Alfred?"

The new boy lowered his head and said softly, "Yes." D.J. realized the boy was very shy or bashful with other people. But skinny as he was, the boy had not missed a lick of digging into the dessert. He had paid for it with some coins he'd produced from a back pocket of his patched blue jeans. D.J. dug into the ice cream and the boys ate in silence for a while.

Suddenly, there was a clatter in the back room. A man's voice yelled in anger and surprise. Mr. Gurney jerked off his half-glasses and ran back yelling, "What's going on?"

It didn't interest D.J. too much, but the fast-disappearing dish of ice cream did. D.J. dug his spoon into the sweet dessert. Alfred's spoon had finally stopped in midair. Alfred was staring through his thick glasses toward the back room where both boys could hear a commotion.

"D.J.! Come get your bear!"

D.J. glanced out the front door. Koko was nowhere in sight. D.J. jumped off the counter stool. "How in the world did he get loose?" D.J. demanded of Alfred. Both boys ran toward the back room.

A delivery man had placed several round cardboard containers of ice cream just inside the open door while he returned to the truck for a second load. The cub had entered the door, knocked over the ice cream containers, and stuck his nose in one where the lid had popped off.

D.J. pulled the cub out. Koko raised his black muzzle with the white-tipped nose smeared with pink ice cream. "You bad bear!" D.J. spoke firmly, as he would have to his dog. "Outside!"

He pulled on the short length of chain which was all that remained of the longer one with which D.J. had tied the cub. "I'm sorry, Mr. Gurney. Somehow he broke his chain. I'll pay you for the ice cream soon's I get some money."

"Forget it, D.J.! But if I were you, from now on I'd keep an eye on that cub! You may be raising an ice cream addict!" Mr. Gurney laughed and bent to help the ice cream delivery man clean up the mess.

Alfred walked through the side door and onto the

tree-lined sidewalk with D.J. "I'd better get Koko back to Dad's pickup before the cub gets into any more mischief," D.J. said.

"I'll walk with you," Alfred replied.

Before they reached the pickup, D.J. learned that Alfred was 12 years old and had just moved to Stoney Ridge from Red Dog, a ghost town in the Mother Lode. Alfred had two older married sisters and a married brother.

"But I've got a little brother still at home. His name is Ralph, but he's always tagging along, so we call him Tag. He's a pain," Alfred concluded.

Alfred added that he lived with his mother and father in a house back off the road. Mr. Milford worked on the green chain* gang at the lumber mill.

D.J. noticed that in the drugstore, Alfred was shy and quiet. But with D.J., Alfred "talked a blue streak," as Grandpa would have said. D.J. figured maybe that Alfred was very sensitive about his poor eyesight. But D.J. and Alfred had instantly liked each other. For more years than he could remember, D.J. had wanted a best friend. Of course, Alfred didn't look like the kind of friend D.J. had wanted, but *any* friend was better than no friend.

D.J. put the cub against the front wheel of the pickup to keep him from wandering into the road. D.J. turned just as his father came out of the mercantile store with a box of groceries.

"Dad, this is Alfred, a new kid in town. Lives half a mile from us on the Limekiln Ditch. Can I go visit him tomorrow?"

Dad never let D.J. go many places. Dad claimed most people didn't keep tight enough reins on their

kids, and they were all troublemakers. But Dad
looked at the skinny kid with the thick eyeglasses
and saw at once he wasn't the troublemaking kind.

"We'll try it once and see how it goes," Dad said,
sliding behind the steering wheel. "Now get that
bear inside and let's go home."

It only took the boys a moment to agree on a
time, and then D.J. waved back at Alfred until the
pickup turned the corner.

Dad drove silently. D.J. glanced at him and saw
the black anger showing there.

Soon Dad started in "cussing and caving," as
Mom used to say. D.J. didn't want to ask why because Dad might get mad at him and change his
mind about either keeping the cub or going to visit
Alfred. But Dad was in no mood to keep his
thoughts to himself.

"That woman is going to drive me out of my
mind!" Dad exclaimed.

D.J. didn't have to ask, "What woman?" He knew
Dad meant Hannah Higgins, the widow of a man
who had once set chokes in the woods with Dad.
Mr. Higgins had been killed in a logging accident.
Mrs. Higgins' daughter was nine-year-old Priscilla.
She always threw dirt clods at D.J. and generally
made his life miserable. He didn't like her, especially since she'd told him that her mother was
thinking of maybe marrying D.J.'s father.

Dad ranted on, driving hard, making the pickup's
tires squeal. "I ran into Hannah in the grocery
store. But she's changed! She only wants to talk
about church, and kept inviting me to go too!"

D.J. didn't see where that was such a terrible

thing, but it reminded him that he hadn't yet told his father about his own commitment to Christ. It had happened while D.J. had been chasing Ol' Satchel Foot. Now didn't seem like the time to say anything.

Dad slapped the steering wheel with the palm of his powerful right hand. "It's all that Paul Stagg's fault! You know that, D.J.? That lay preacher is turning this town into a revival camp! I want you to stay away from him! You hear? And stay away from that red-headed daughter of his too!"

D.J. didn't need any encouragement on that score. He had never met anybody who was so spunky as Kathy Stagg. She was also quick to tell him what she thought about almost anything. That almost always was not what D.J. thought, so he and Kathy usually made the sparks fly when they talked very long.

"Yes, Dad," he said, not wanting to upset his plans for tomorrow. He added, "I like Alfred. Maybe he and I could get to be best friends. You suppose?"

Dad didn't hear. He pressed the pedal to the floor and roared out of Stoney Ridge and into the scenic mountain country. He barely slowed to ease the pick-up across the little creek that separated the Dillons' rented house from the paved county road. The hounds came out from under the porch and bayed Dad and D.J.'s approach. Grandpa had been dozing on the porch, but he glanced up from his cane-bottom chair and waved his Irish shillelagh in greeting.

A few minutes later D.J. fed the cub in the kitchen. Then the boy walked out the back side door from the kitchen and got the cracklings* to feed the hounds. He fed Hero, patting him absently, then moved on to feed the other dogs. Outside the only window from the living room, D.J. heard Dad. He was still ranting and cussing angrily, his voice easily heard through the open window. Grandpa's voice was unusually calm.

"Sam, why don't you be honest with yourself for a change? That widder woman fills a big hole in your life. The sooner you admit it and ask her to marry you, the sooner you'll quit fighting the world."

D.J. stopped scraping cracklings into a hound's pan. He straightened up in surprise.

Dad swore something fierce, but Grandpa's voice was still calm. "I know it's not been quite a year since your wife got killed, Sam, but you're not the bachelor type. And my grandson needs a mother's hand too."

D.J. wanted to yell, "No! I don't want any mother but my own, and she's dead!" But he didn't say anything as Dad and Grandpa moved away inside the house.

Slowly, the boy lifted his eyes to the conifers, past the evergreens' slender tips and even past the great white summer clouds that marked a distant thunderhead. "Lord, I know that I recently gave my life to You, but please—don't let my dad marry Mrs. Higgins! I can hardly stand that daughter of hers!"

But the moment D.J. whispered the words, he had the feeling that prayer was not going to be answered. He shuddered even though it was late July.

Chapter Three

ALFRED LEADS THE CUB INTO TROUBLE

After doing his chores the next morning, D.J. walked around the east side of the house where the hounds were chained. Except for the first day after the cub was brought home, the hounds had ignored the bear. The female trail hound had even allowed Koko to sleep with her pups. D.J. found it strange that such a thing would happen with natural enemies, but Koko didn't seem like a wild animal at all. He seemed born to live with people.

D.J. reached into the dog house and pulled Koko out. The pups tumbled out after the bear, ready for a romp. But the boy was anxious to see his new friend, Alfred. D.J. snapped a chain on the cub. D.J.'s hair-pulling bear dog, Hero, whined and stood on his hind legs, held back by his collar and chain. He was very anxious to go with D.J. For a moment, the boy hesitated. Then he decided he'd better take the cub alone so Alfred could help train Koko.

The boy started around the corner of the porch.
He heard Grandpa's rocking chair squeaking.
"Grandpa, Dad said I could go over to see a new
kid named Alfred. Lives on Limekiln Ditch. I'll be
home before supper."

Grandpa didn't answer. D.J. stopped, suddenly
aware that Grandpa was rocking very fast. He only
did that when he was angry. D.J. started to call a
warning, but it was too late. Grandpa's fast rocking
had tilted the old red cane-bottom chair so far
backward that it suddenly went on over. Grandpa
was thrown out onto the splintery porch with a
crash. The old man rolled over, grabbed his Irish
shillelagh, and began whacking on the toppled
chair. Just as suddenly, Grandpa stopped.

D.J. started to run up on the porch, but the old
man sat up, found his bifocal glasses, and resettled
them on his nose. He shoved himself to his feet
with his blackthorn cane and shook his head. "Now
I know how the Apostle Paul felt when he said he
did things he didn't want to do!"

"You hurt, Grandpa?"

"No, D.J. —just mad. And I shouldn't be. But I get
so all-fired burned up at your father sometimes!
He's so stubborn! Then I get mad at myself for getting mad at him because if I'm this new creation
Paul the Apostle talks about, then I shouldn't get
mad at anybody! Isn't that so, D.J.?"

The boy grinned. "Grandpa, you need to ask Paul
Stagg about such things. I'm having trouble telling
Dad about what I decided to do with my life when
Ol' Satchel Foot had me up a tree."

The old man brushed a liver-spotted hand across

his thin gray hair. He let D.J. help him set the rocker upright. Grandpa lowered himself slowly into the chair. "I suppose you're a'going to make a body guess what you done, D.J.?"

"Don't mean to, Grandpa, but I guess I'm a little unsure how to do it. I mean, tell people I gave my life to the Lord. Only you did that in a church, like most people, while I did it up a tree with a mad bear trying to eat my foot off."

Grandpa cackled with glee. "Well, now! You don't say! Two of us Christians in this house, now, eh? Your mother would be mighty happy! But how come you didn't say anything?"

"Scared of what Dad would say, I guess. I've even been afraid he'd get mad if he saw me reading Mom's old Bible."

The old man laughed, throwing back his head so his bifocals slipped on his nose. "Now, don't that beat all? I been having trouble reading the Bible too, but mostly because I can't see too good, even with these spectacles! Tell you what, D.J. Let's you and me read the Scriptures together!"

"I'd like that, Grandpa."

"Good! We'll do it! Well, you'd best get along with your bear and meet your new friend."

For a moment, D.J. hesitated. He knew why Grandpa was mad at Dad because the boy had overheard their conversation the night before. But was that enough to make Grandpa still be mad this morning?

The boy asked, "You think Dad will ask Mrs. Higgins to marry him, Grandpa?"

"He might. Would that bother you?"

D.J. shrugged. "Guess so, Grandpa. She's nice
enough, but nobody can take my mother's place.
Besides, she's got a mean daughter who's always
getting me in trouble."

"You don't want Pris for a stepsister?"

"No, Grandpa, I don't."

The old man sighed. "Guess maybe I'd better
study on that a while. Maybe pray too. Well, now
you run along and have fun with that there cub."

* * * * *

Alfred's house had a tin roof with long rust spots
where the snow and rain had made long ugly
slashes. The house was small and built up high
with several steps going up to the front door. The
garage was under the house. A dark-green yew tree
stood to the right side of the white house. A sugar
pine stood to the left. D.J. tied the bear cub to the
bottom post on the stairs and clumped heavily up
to knock on the door.

A pleasant woman with sad brown eyes opened
the door. Her mouse-colored hair was parted in the
middle and tied back in a bun. She wore thick
glasses like her son. She looked rather prim and
proper, like a schoolteacher Dad talked about having when he was a boy.

"I'm D.J. Dillon," the boy said. "I came to see
Alfred."

"D.J.! Come in! Alfred's been expecting you!" She
raised her voice. "Alfred, your friend's here." She
opened the door wide and indicated two old pale-
green upholstered chairs. "I'm Alfred's mother,
Mrs. Milford. Have a seat. He'll be right out. He's
helping his little brother with a puzzle."

"Ralph?"

"Yes, but everyone calls him Tag. My Alfred's very good with puzzles and things. Likes big words. Got two dictionaries. Reads a lot. Tag's been wanting to go with you boys, so we gave him the puzzle to keep him happy."

Mrs. Milford could also talk a blue streak, D.J. thought. Sometimes lonely people did that when they had company, he'd noticed. Grandpa did it once in a while. D.J. took the nearest green chair and glanced around the room. Boxes were partly unpacked. Some were opened and some still closed. The room had pale-pink rose wallpaper. Countless pictures in frames were already hanging on the walls or placed on top of every flat piece of furniture. The lace curtains had been hung. D.J. figured Mrs. Milford was a real homebody.

"My Alfred tells me you have a bear cub?"

D.J. shifted in his chair. "Yes'm."

"Doesn't your mother think that's dangerous?"

"She's dead."

"Oh! I'm sorry."

"It's OK. A drunken driver hit her and another woman from church last winter. They were driving on that narrow stretch of mountain road between Stoney Ridge and Indian Springs."

Mrs. Milford was upset. She twisted her hands together so hard D.J. thought they must hurt. She brushed her hair back nervously. "You live with your father?"

"And Grandpa. Dad's father."

"I see. You like school, D.J.?"

"Sometimes."

D.J. didn't know why he was uncomfortable, but he was glad when he heard Alfred hurrying down the narrow hallway from a back bedroom.

"Hi," Alfred said, flopping onto the other green chair. "You bring your cub?"

"Tied at the foot of the steps."

"Mom, can we bring him into the house?"

"Mercy, no! A wild animal like that? I'm not even sure I should let you play with him. Maybe I'd better take a look at him before I decide for sure."

She walked to the front door, opened it, and looked down. D.J. and Alfred exchanged glances. Each was a little unsure of what Mrs. Milford would decide. In a moment, she stepped back in and closed the door.

"I had a cat bigger than that little bear," she announced. "I suppose it's OK. But Alfred, you don't do anything that'll upset your father."

Alfred stood, fairly grinning. "I won't, Mom."

"And be home for lunch. D.J., you'll join us, of course."

The boy nodded, thanked her for the luncheon invitation, and then followed his new friend out the front door and down the steps. Koko had been trying to climb the post to which he was chained. D.J. picked up the cub and carried him down to the ground where the boy released him.

"Can I hold him?" Alfred asked.

"Sure. But go slow at first."

"I've been studying up on California black bears since yesterday," the new boy announced, slowly extending the back of his hand to the cub.

"Oh?"

"Yes. There are two races of black bears in this state. The northwestern black bear — called *Ursus americanus altifrontails* — and the Sierra Nevada black bear, which this one is. They inhabit the Cascade, Klamath, North and South Coastal mountains, plus what's called the Peninsular and Sierra Nevada mountain ranges from near sea level to about 3,000 meters. Since a meter is the same as 39.37 United States inches, that's about. . . ."

D.J. interrupted with a laugh. "Hey, wait! I'll take your word for everything! Boy! You must be a brain."

Alfred's face sobered. He lowered his eyes. "Please don't call me that," he said quietly.

"Call you what?"

"A *brain.* That's what kids called me at the last school, and nobody wanted me to play with them. They were mean about my glasses too."

D.J. stared at his new friend. It was plain that Alfred was very sensitive about what he was and what people thought he was. "Alfred, as far as I'm concerned, you're my friend. Now, I want to be a writer, and writers have to know lots of things. But nobody calls me a — well, you and I are friends, and that's that."

Alfred's grin was wide as a slice of picnic-cut watermelon. "And can Koko be my friend too?"

"Ask him!"

The new boy nodded and bent to slowly take the cub's right forepaw. "Koko, are we friends? We are? Let's shake on it!"

Alfred stood, all smiles. "He licked me! Did you see that? He likes me!"

"Or maybe he was tasting you first to see if he

wanted to eat you," D.J. said, trying to keep a straight face.

Alfred shook his head. "Black bears are shy omnivorous* mammals, so they'll eat all kinds of foods, but they don't eat people! You knew that, didn't you?"

"Yes, I was just teasing," D.J. admitted with a grin.

For a moment, Alfred considered that. "But it's not mean teasing, like most kids. You're teasing like friends."

"Like friends," D.J. admitted.

Alfred said, "I never had a real friend before. I mean, except for books and trees."

"Me, either," D.J. admitted, smiling happily. Then he frowned. "Books and trees?"

"My best friends up to now," Alfred said owlishly.

D.J. freed the bear's chain from the post and then handed the chain to Alfred. "You can lead him first."

Alfred's mouth dropped open. His chin bobbed and he swallowed twice, real fast and hard, before he asked, "Can I?"

"Sure."

"First, let me take him down to the store and show him to Mrs. Greenlee. Then we'll go exploring. OK?"

"OK!"

They started to run down the hill toward the combination grocery store and service station. The store was an off-shade of white with green trim and a red composition roof. D.J. stopped and puffed a little as he asked, "How can trees be friends?"

"Trees never hurt your feelings," Alfred said, pulling the cub's chain and easing the little bear into a "heel" position against his left leg. "And trees are always nice. As friends should be."

"Oh," D.J. said softly. "I never thought of it like that."

"Of course," Alfred said, starting to run again and looking back to see how easily the cub was following, "I'd rather have a real live human friend like you."

"Me too!" D.J. agreed.

Alfred pushed open the door to the little store, making a cowbell clang above the door. D.J. caught the smell of wooden floors cleaned with sawdust and some kind of chemical. Racks of fishing poles and lures took up the whole right side of the store. Narrow aisles of groceries with a tiny meat counter filled the left side.

Alfred whispered, "Mrs. Greenlee will sure be surprised! Oh, hi, Mrs. Greenlee! Look what I got!"

The proprietor* was a big woman with arms that jiggled between her elbows and shoulders. It was cool and semi-dark in the store, but D.J. could see she was perspiring.

"What is that thing, Alfred?" Mrs. Greenlee asked. She produced a pair of black-rimmed glasses from her apron pocket and adjusted them. "My stars! It's a bear!"

"Just a cub, really, Mrs. Green—"

"Get that thing out of here!" She pointed a heavy hand with stiff forefinger. "Out! OUT!"

The woman's voice made the cub back up suddenly. D.J. saw what was going to happen, but Alfred was looking in surprise at the woman. He didn't tighten the chain. D.J. jumped to grab the bear as the woman continued to yell, her voice getting higher every second.

The cub backed into a display rack of fishing poles. They clattered to the floor. Koko reacted by jumping away. His nose smashed into a stack of canned peaches. The cans gave slightly, offering the cub a kind of cave. He pushed hard into it, bringing down the entire display with a terrible crash.

"Out! OUT! **OUT!**" Mrs. Greenlee shrieked.

D.J. bent and scooped the cub into his arms just before the bear smashed into an open pickle barrel. D.J. ran for the door with Alfred trying to apologize and walk backward at the same time. He tripped over a loose peach can that had rolled halfway to the door. Alfred fell like a scarecrow, outstretched arms flying. They hit a stack of soap boxes. As the display crumpled slowly and the woman covered her eyes, Alfred scooted out the door.

D.J. didn't know why, but he was running, hugging the bear to his chest. When he reached the foot of Alfred's front steps, D.J. stopped to catch his breath. Alfred clumped up in his big boots and flopped down heavily beside him.

D.J. whistled. "Whoowee! She was mad!"

"No reason to be," Alfred said, looking at the store as if he expected Mrs. Greenlee to be chasing them. "Guess she doesn't like surprises much."

D.J. thought a minute. "Maybe we'd better go offer to clean up things. But we'll leave the bear here."

Alfred grinned. "Good idea! Boy! I like having a friend! Especially when you've got a bear cub! Hey! I can just tell this is going to be a year neither of us will ever forget!"

D.J. swallowed hard. Somehow, he had a feeling Alfred was right, and it sort of scared him.

Chapter Four

A SCARE FOR D.J.

D.J. knew something was wrong when he came within sight of his home late that afternoon.

Grandpa Dillon was waiting in the shade of the Lombardy poplars across the creek. The old man tucked his pocket New Testament into the front of his bib overalls and waved. The boy waved back. He couldn't hear above the noisy waters gurgling over stones. He quickly removed his shoes and socks, tied the shoelaces together and swung the shoes around his neck. He picked up Koko in his arms and hurriedly waded across the creek.

"Something wrong, Grandpa?" the boy asked, putting the cub gently on the bank and tightening his grip on the chain.

The old man snorted and pounded his black-thorn cane on the small stones beside the creek. "Your father's been ranting and raving ever since he got home from work."

D.J. felt fear shoot through his body. "What about? Dad hear about what Koko did in the little store?"

"No, not that. But what'd the cub do?"

"Nothing serious. Besides, Alfred and I cleaned it up. What about Dad?"

"The mill's threatening to go on strike, and that'd mean there'd be no need for choke-setters in the timber. Your father would be out of work."

"Maybe they won't strike," the boy said hopefully. "They threatened to do that a couple years ago, but they didn't. Remember?"

"Just the same, I thought I'd come down and warn you so's you don't rile him none."

"I'll be careful. And thanks, Grandpa. Come on, Koko."

Dad looked up when the boy entered the side door into the kitchen. "You're late getting to your chores, D.J."

"I'll get them done fast."

"No supper till you do."

"I know." D.J. put the bear on the floor.

"And another thing: you can't go off and leave that dog anymore. He's been whining and carrying on because you left him."

"I thought it'd be best to only take the cub."

"Well, you thought *wrong!* You wanted both the dog and the bear, so you take them *both* with you! Is that clear?"

"Yes, sir."

"Now get to those chores. And then take a bath. We're driving into town."

"Tonight?"

"Yes, tonight!"

D.J. had a sickening feeling he knew why, yet he tried to think how to find out without asking. "But won't all the stores be closed?"

"Not going to any store! We're going to see Hannah Higgins and her little Priscilla!"

"Ah, Dad!"

"And you be nice to that little girl or I'll larrup you good, even if you are near-on to man-size! You hear me?"

"Yes, sir."

Grandpa came into the bathroom where D.J. was. The old man whispered, "A man needs to talk to a woman sometimes, especially when he's hurt, like your father is now over the strike thing. He'll be OK."

An hour later, the boy felt uncomfortable in his only good white shirt which was already too short for him. His arms stuck out a good two inches from the sleeves. The collar was tight and scratchy. Grandpa had tied a four-in-hand knot in an old red and green necktie which was long out of style and seemed about to choke D.J. His brown pants came to the top of his only good pair of high top oxblood* shoes, which he had polished with an old rag. Even so, the scuff marks showed and the shoes pinched because the boy had outgrown them.

Dad wore a yellow bow tie with tiny black dots, a lime green cowboy shirt with fancy embroidery, a clean pair of blue jeans, and black low-cut shoes. They looked like the ones he used to wear in the navy, and he had "spit polished" them the way he had back then. Mom used to say Dad had many good qualities, but choosing good clothes combinations wasn't one of them. She had always laid out his clothes for funerals and weddings and other special events.

Dad didn't explain why they were going to see Mrs. Higgins, but D.J. had a sick feeling Dad really wanted to ask her to marry him. Of course, maybe Grandpa was right, and Dad just needed to talk to a woman. Yet the boy doubted that. D.J. didn't want his father to remarry, but the boy knew better than to say anything when Dad was in one of his black moods.

Priscilla Higgins opened the door to Dad's knock. She flipped on the porch light though it wasn't quite dark yet.

"MOM! It's Mr. Dillon and Davey!"

Priscilla's shriek went through the boy's body like a fishhook through a thumb. He didn't like being called "Davey" anymore, either. It was much too babyish, he thought. Everyone had started calling him D.J. or David, except Pris. The boy thought she did it on purpose because he didn't like it.

Mrs. Higgins didn't come until her daughter shrieked twice more. D.J. could hear quick movements back in the house and guessed the widow was doing something before coming out. Dad was nervously twisting one of the embroidered flowers on the front of his cowboy shirt. He tried to look through the screen door. As Dad looked across the living room toward the back of the house, D.J. saw Pris look at him and make a face. She was always doing that, and nobody ever caught her.

Finally Mrs. Higgins walked briskly through the living room and toward the front door. She was still touching up her short blond hair. Her blue eyes lit up. She was sort of pretty, in a way.

She smiled and said, "Sam, D.J., what a surprise!"

"I had to see you, Hannah," Dad said softly. He had shaved and smelled of too much after-shave lotion. "Am I — are we — interrupting anything?"

"No, Sam! Pris and I were just finishing up the supper dishes. But there's a little lemon meringue pie left, and I could put on a pot of coffee."

"No, thanks," Dad answered.

D.J. glanced up at his father in real surprise. Since Dad had started calling on Mrs. Higgins, he always arrived in time for supper. She was one of the best cooks in Stoney Ridge, and her house was always neat and clean, even if she did have a hard time living on a widow's pension. The boy couldn't imagine turning down dessert.

"No pie, Sam? Well, how about you, D.J.?"

The boy's mouth almost ached with the remembered taste of Mrs. Higgins' pies, but a glance at his father told him to say no. "Thank you kindly, but I've had supper and dessert."

"My stars! Where are my manners? Come in! Come in! Priscilla, you can let the rest of the dishes dry by themselves. Sam, D.J., sit down. Make yourselves to home."

"Thank you, Hannah, but if it's all the same to you, I'll stand."

"My! Something important happen?"

"No; leastwise, not yet. D.J., why don't you let Pris show you the flowers in the yard?"

The girl shook her head. "Getting too dark, Mr. Dillon."

Mrs. Higgins said firmly, "Take a flashlight, Pris."

D.J. stayed well away from the little girl as she led him outside. This was the longest time he'd ever been around her without her kicking him on the shins or throwing a dirt clod at him.

Mom used to say Priscilla was just seeking attention because she was an only child. D.J. didn't believe that because he was also an only child and he didn't seek attention that way.

Pris seemed unusually quiet. She led the way along the concrete sidewalk, past the roses and the pansy beds toward the backyard. D.J. watched carefully, but the little girl didn't reach for anything to throw at him. She sat down on the back step and clasped her hands around her knees.

"You know what it means when big folks make us kids go outside, don't you?"

D.J. leaned against the back of the house and asked, "What does it mean?"

"It means something important they don't want us to hear."

"Such as?"

"Such as the women at the church being right."

"About what?"

"Your dad marrying my mother."

"Where'd you ever get a crazy notion like that?"

"It's not crazy! I told you once what they said. My mother and your father aren't like us kids. They need somebody else. That's what the church women said. And my mother agrees."

D.J. was feeling a sickness creeping over him. He swallowed hard, but didn't say anything.

Pris continued, "But she's not going to marry him."

The boy pushed himself away from the house. "What makes you say that?"

"Because, since Paul Stagg came to pastor our church, Mom's been going there all the time; even to prayer meeting."

"So?" D.J. challenged.

"Mom says a Christian shouldn't marry someone who's not a believer. It has something to do with what the church women call 'not being unevenly yoked together.' I heard Mother telling some of the women at the quilting and Bible study last week that she'd made up her mind."

D.J. snapped, "He hasn't even asked her! Maybe he never will! Besides, he's not told me he's going to do such a thing!"

The little girl shrugged and scuffed her heel on the back sidewalk. "She wouldn't, even if he did."

D.J. was ready to shout with happiness. "You sure?"

"Positive! If he asks her, she's going to turn him down flat."

D.J. was ready to jump about on the small, neat lawn, but he held himself in check. Then another thought hit him, and the boy felt his insides grow cold. If Dad *did* ask Mrs. Higgins to marry him, and she said no, Dad was going to be so mad there'd be no reasoning with him.

Pris jumped up. "Listen!"

D.J. cocked his head. Dad's voice was rising angrily in the still evening air.

"Oh, oh!" Pris said softly.

"Yeah," D.J. agreed.

In a moment, the boy and girl exchanged glances

as the front door slammed shut and heavy footsteps sounded rapidly across the small wooden porch. D.J. turned to Pris. "He may even forget he brought me!" He started to run.

"Bye!" Pris called after him.

The boy ran fast and slid into the front seat of the pickup just as Dad started the motor and slammed the truck into gear. The pickup jerked away from the curb so hard that the boy's neck snapped against the backseat cushion. Dad didn't seem to even notice his son was beside him.

"That preacher!" Dad exploded, pounding the steering wheel with his open right hand. "It's all his fault! I'm going to teach him to stay out of other people's business!"

D.J. had seen what his father's violent temper could do when he got mad at another grown-up. The boy's lips moved silently. *O Lord, Paul Stagg's a nice man! Please don't let my father hurt him!*

Chapter Five

A FILM COMPANY IS COMING

D.J. sighed quietly with relief when he saw a strange car parked in the driveway behind Paul Stagg's old sedan. Dad swore viciously and stopped at the curb, his headlights on the new vehicle.

"He's got company!" Dad exploded.

"Don't recognize the car," D.J. said. "Brand new. Got some kind of a sign on the side."

"Take the flashlight and run and see what it says."

"Ah, Dad, couldn't we just go home?"

Dad roared into a long string of angry words that burned the boy's ears. Even though he'd been hearing them as long as he could remember, the violent anger in the words always made D.J. draw back. Quickly he jumped out of the pickup, ran in the headlights to the vehicle, and shined Dad's five-cell flashlight on the sign painted on the front passenger's side. D.J. hurried back to the pickup and climbed into the high cab.

"It says, 'Quality Film Production Corporation.' I think that's the movie company that made some of the pictures Mom took me to at church last year."

Dad ran his strong brown right hand over his chin. "Why would they be here?"

"Maybe they're going to shoot a movie. I've heard about other companies shooting near here."

"Even if they were, why would they be stopped at Paul Stagg's house?"

"I don't know," D.J. admitted. "But if they do shoot a movie here, do you suppose I could get a part? I've heard about that. They're called 'extras,' and sometimes the Chamber of Commerce in Indian Springs helps find local people to be in those movies. If they do, could I?"

Dad interrupted, "Somebody's coming out!"

Paul Stagg's big body filled the doorway. He held the screen open while a well-dressed man in a lightweight summer suit stepped onto the porch. The man was almost handsome, D.J. thought. Mrs. Stagg followed the men onto the porch. A moment later, Kathy stepped outside.

D.J. whispered, "Are we going to leave, Dad?"

"Can't figure who that feller is or what he's doing here," Dad said. His voice was calm. The anger had given way to curiosity.

"Oh! Oh!" D.J. said. "Here comes Paul!"

The boy hoped Dad would put the pickup into reverse and back out, but he waited. In a moment, the giant of a man had walked past the headlights and was leaning forward to peer into the driver's side of the pickup. "I'm still half-blind from the lights," the big man rumbled pleasantly, "but I do believe I recognize the Dillon family."

"You got that right," Dad said. His voice was still calm.

"Sam! Welcome." The lay preacher stuck out his right hand and took Dad's. "D.J., glad to see you too. Well, now, what brings you two here?"

D.J. held his breath, but Dad kept calm. "Nothing that won't keep," Dad said. "I see you got company."

"Get out and meet him," Paul rumbled pleasantly. "That's Jay Calkins, and he's scouting for locations to shoot a family-type film next spring."

In a moment, Dad was shaking hands with the filmmaker. Mr. Calkins also reached out his right hand and shook D.J.'s hand. "Say, young man, you look like the type who'd like to have a small part in a family film. Am I right?"

D.J. gulped and nodded. "Sure would!"

"Well, this young lady here . . . Kathy, is it? Yes, Kathy! Well, she's probably going to do a walk-on too. While we won't be shooting until next spring, if you talk to Mr. Stagg here, I'm pretty sure something can be arranged. Mr. Stagg's going to be our contact man since I worked with him some years ago when we had a 'shoot' on location near where he used to live."

The man spoke very rapidly, the words flowing through a smile that never seemed to fade. D.J. had always had a little suspicious feeling about moviemakers, but he liked Mr. Calkins. Maybe it was because he made films that could be shown in churches.

Suddenly, D.J. had an idea. "Mr. Calkins, could my bear have a part in your movie?"

The man had started to talk to Dad and the other adults, but he stopped and bent to look straight into the boy's eyes. "You've got a bear?"

"A cub. But he's real smart and can learn any trick or do anything by the time you're ready to make your movie." D.J. felt excitement flowing through him like hot chocolate on a wintry night.

"Well, now, that's very interesting, D.J.! Very interesting! You see, this movie is about a man who loves children and animals, especially bears. We've already contracted for a bear through the man who owns the animal. But maybe we can work out something so your cub can appear in a background shot or something. Paul," the man continued, straightening again to look up at the tall lay preacher, "remind me of this conversation when we return for the shoot."

*   *   *   *   *

The rest of the summer rushed by so fast D.J. could hardly believe it. The tall sugar pines developed cones high on the branches where they perched openly, tempting squirrels. Wild sweet pea vines produced pale pink and white blossoms that clung to the open spots of ground away from the sugar pines and closer to the ponderosas. Fawns, born with spots which helped hide them from enemies, slowly turned a solid, soft brown like their mothers. Crested jays screamed at real and imaginary dangers as their eggs were laid, hatched, and the young birds began trying their wings. The days were warm and the nights were brisk for sleeping.

D.J. had only two problems. The first was Nails Abst, who never gave up his claim to the bear cub.

Twice in town the older boy saw D.J. and the cub and tried to take the cub away.

"You stole my bear," Nails said the first time. "I want him back."

"He's not your bear!"

"He's mine, and you'd better give him over right now!"

Nails reached out suddenly and jerked the cub's lead chain from D.J.'s hands. The older boy yanked so hard on the chain that the bear's neck was stretched. The cub squealed and swatted at Nails' pants leg, ripping it.

"Hey! You cut that out! I'll take a club to you!"

The incident ended suddenly when Paul Stagg came out of the barbershop and spoke sternly to the older boy. Nails made a nasty remark and left, threatening to get D.J. and the cub the next time they were alone.

D.J. didn't really like to go to Stoney Ridge with his father anymore. But when they were buying groceries one Saturday afternoon, D.J. carried a box to the pickup. It was too hot to leave the cub in the cab, so D.J. had tied Koko to a light post. Two town dogs rushed up to sniff the cub. Instantly, he turned and swatted them both so hard they yelped and ran off with their tails tucked. D.J. recognized one hound as the Absts'. By the time D.J. had put the box of groceries in the pickup, Nails came running down the street.

"You kicked my dog, D.J. Dillon!"

"I didn't touch your dog!"

"I saw his shoulder! He's cut up from where you kicked him!"

"I didn't come near your dog!"

Nails hesitated, his eyes lighting on the bear. The cub was looking at him and making little huffing sounds. D.J. had never heard Koko do that before.

Nails' eyes narrowed. "It was that bear then! Yeah, that's it! You sicked that bear on him! And that's *my* bear. Hand him over!"

"Now, Nails, you know I can't do that!"

"Why not?"

"Because he's *my* cub, that's why!"

"That's not the real reason! I heard about that movie man saying he needed a bear for his picture next spring, and you're fixing to make money off my cub!"

"That's not what the man said, and besides. . . . "

Tinsley Abst, Nails' father, came out of the little community garage two doors down and yelled, "Nails, the pickup's fixed! Let's go!"

D.J. watched the older boy leave, knowing that sooner or later there was going to be real trouble over the cub. D.J. remembered how he'd saved Nails' life when the outlaw bear, Ol' Satchel Foot, caught Nails at Mad River in Devil's Slide Canyon. But it didn't seem to mean anything to Nails.

D.J. told Alfred one day, "I'm never going to give up Koko to Nails! He'll hurt him! But I don't know what to do!"

"It'll work out," Alfred said. "That's what my folks are always saying to me. It'll work out."

"I hope so," D.J. said fervently.

D.J.'s second problem was more personal. He still hadn't been able to tell his dad about the decision he'd made in the tree with that Ol' Satchel

Foot trying to get him. To make a Christian commitment had been so easy, but to "give witness," as
Paul Stagg had put it, was the hardest thing D.J.
had ever tried to do.

Sometimes D.J. and Grandpa read the Bible
together, but never when Dad was home. D.J. managed to read his mother's Bible every day when he
went out to his favorite ponderosa tree. That was
where he usually tried to write stories to practice
being an author. However, the boy felt he was
sneaky in his Bible reading, as though he were
ashamed. He wasn't, but he just didn't have the
courage to speak up about his faith. It began to give
him a guilty conscience.

"Sometimes I think God will 'get me' for that,"
D.J. told Alfred one day when they were fishing for
rainbow trout in the ditch that carried the town's
drinking water down from the higher mountains.

Alfred couldn't remember when he wasn't a
Christian. "Mom says God doesn't 'get you' for
things when you're trying to do right."

"Well, I'm trying hard, but it's bothering me a
whole lot about not telling Dad. Mom used to try
talking to him about Jesus all the time, and Dad
always got mad. He's liable to thump me pretty good
if he thinks I've done something he doesn't like."

"You'll tell him," Alfred said, reeling in a 15-inch
fighting rainbow.

D.J. wasn't sure. He continued to read the Bible
under the tree where for two years he had been
trying to write short stories with a lead pencil.
Sometimes he went to Sunday School and church
when somebody stopped by to give him a ride. He

thought about talking to Paul Stagg about his being afraid to witness to people, but grown-ups were always crowded around the preacher at church, and D.J. never saw him alone.

Dad was mad all the time. Sometimes D.J. heard him cussing the preacher for making Hannah Higgins turn him down. But Dad hadn't said anything more about getting even with Paul Stagg. Dad was also mad because the mill strike seemed more and more certain, and that would throw him out of work as a choke-setter. But it hadn't happened yet.

During that summer D.J. and Alfred explored the mountains, the creeks, the ditches, and everything else they could find. D.J. always took the cub and the little hair-pulling bear dog along. Hero, the dog, always stayed close to the boy's side. Alfred usually got to lead Koko on his chain. D.J. recognized something was happening to Alfred, but he didn't know what it was until one day at Alfred's home.

Mrs. Milford handed D.J. two sack lunches while he stood at the top of the steep stairs waiting for Alfred. She said, "D.J., I've been wanting to thank you for letting my boy lead that bear so often when you boys are out fooling around."

"It's nothing, Mrs. Milford. I've got my dog, and it's too hard to keep their chains from getting tangled if one person tries to lead both animals."

"Whatever the reason, you're making my Alfred into a different boy. Have you noticed? He's always been shy, but he's different around that bear."

"He speaks right up to people, Mrs. Milford. Fact is, he goes up to them when we meet somebody on the trails and he shows them the bear."

"That's what I mean, D.J. Alfred wasn't like that until he met you, and I doubt he'd be like that unless the cub was along."

D.J. remembered the first time they'd taken the cub down the hill to the little store. The minute Alfred had taken the cub's chain, he had wanted to show off that bear.

Mrs. Milford went on, "Why, when he was too young to go to school, he used to hide behind my skirts when anybody came by. Of course, we lived away back in the country off the road, and people rarely visited."

"Sort of like me, I guess. We live so far out that there's not even a real driveway up to our place."

Mrs. Milford was looking up at the yew tree, but D.J. didn't think she was seeing it. She was remembering. "Alfred was so shy that when he finally started school, he cried for days! In fact, he carried on until we thought for a while he'd never adjust. When he finally did, he was not very sociable and the kids were sometimes cruel to him. That's partly because he has to wear those glasses."

"Well, he's doing fine now," D.J. assured her.

"I know. But I hope it continues when school opens."

"We'll be best friends in school, same as this summer."

"But the bear won't be with you in school, and I'm not sure what that will do to my boy. But everything will turn out all right, I'm sure."

The remaining weeks of summer, the cub gained weight so fast D.J. figured Koko would be near a hundred pounds by spring when the movie was made.

The cub slept at the foot of D.J.'s rollaway bed in the kitchen until Koko developed a midnight hunger.

D.J. was half-asleep the first night he heard the cub jump down from the bed and pad over to the low cupboard near the sink where Grandpa kept his canned goods. The boy was already fully asleep again when he heard a crash. D.J. sat up in bed. In the pale moonlight through the window, he saw Koko holding a big can of peaches. D.J. knew that's what they were by the fragrance. The cub's strong foreclaws had ripped the can open. He held the can between both forepaws and tipped the sweet fruit halves into his open mouth.

"No, Koko! No!" D.J. whispered as firmly as he could, hoping not to awaken Dad or Grandpa. But Dad was already running across the faded linoleum floor from his bedroom. He snapped on the light and exploded at the mess.

"That bear!" Dad thundered. "That bear is getting too big to roam loose! Put him on a chain or keep him outside with the hounds!"

"Ah, Dad, he didn't mean any harm!"

"I said chain that bear or else put him outside! Then you clean up that mess! If the bear starts doing things like that, you'll have to get rid of him!"

D.J. stopped dead still. Dad's words went through the boy's body like a pain. Until that moment, he'd not realized how much he had come to care about that fast-growing cub. But there was no doubt in the boy's mind, either: if the cub got into too much trouble, Dad would make D.J. get rid of his pet.

It only took a few days before Koko got into a *real* disaster.

UNINVITED GUEST AT A PICNIC

Stoney Ridge was a workingman's town, so the annual Labor Day picnic was one of the biggest events of the year. Everyone came to the only city park, a block-square area of trees and lawns with an old Shay logging engine display near the comfort stations.

Sam Dillon wore his bright red cowboy shirt with lime green pants, a pair of red and green cowboy boots, and a quality maroon-colored Stetson hat with rolled brim. D.J. couldn't help smiling at the way his father strutted. Even Alfred noticed it.

"Your father looks like one of those little fighting banty roosters," Alfred said, biting into a handful of potato chips.

"I sure hope he doesn't get into a fight," D.J. said thoughtfully. "He's probably still mad at Paul Stagg. Dad blames him for the way Mrs. Higgins turned him down the night he proposed. And when Dad gets mad at somebody, he stays mad until he has a chance to get even."

"A vindictive nature*," Alfred observed owlishly, twisting his head to see the crowd through his thick glasses.

D.J. was surprised to find he was a little bothered by Alfred's use of big words. Though D.J. knew a writer had to understand all kinds of words, he didn't much care for his friend using words he didn't know. He'd have to remember to look that one up. But what bothered D.J. most was the realization he was getting upset over little things.

Alfred's eyes stopped moving over the crowd. "Speaking of getting even, isn't that Nails Abst over by the free soft drink tub?"

D.J. turned to shade his eyes against the sun. "That's him all right. I'm surprised he showed up here."

"Well, at least he can't try to take our cub away from us."

D.J. glanced sharply at his friend. Alfred had always called Koko "your" cub until just now. "Had to leave him home with my dog and the hounds."

"You know, D.J., I've thought of something that worries me a little."

"What's that?"

Alfred stuffed more potato chips into his mouth, chewed noisily, and then swallowed quickly before answering. "What's to keep Nails from stealing Koko?"

"You mean, kidnapping the cub?"

"Why not? I wouldn't put it past him, especially since you won't give the bear up when Nails tries to take him."

That thought had never occurred to D.J. He tried to put the idea out of his mind, but it stuck. Alfred said he was going to get a free soft drink and ran off to the right. D.J. walked over to where Dad was watching the old-time fiddlers practicing under the elm trees. Dad was talking to one of the waitresses where the lumberjacks ate. She chewed her gum with her mouth open and laughed loudly at something Dad said.

D.J. saw Mrs. Higgins nearby, helping tamp* rock salt into the ice cream freezer which some men were turning. She was smiling and talking to the women putting a red-and-white-checkered tablecloth on one of the park tables. Yet the boy saw Mrs. Higgins' eyes flicker to Dad and away.

Suddenly, something struck D.J.'s chest. He glanced down to see a piece of ice bounce from his short-sleeved white sport shirt onto the grass. He turned in time to duck a second piece of ice sailing through the air toward him.

"Priscilla! You cut that out!" D.J.'s voice was louder than he intended.

The moment her hand had released the second piece of ice, the nine-year-old girl had turned away. At the boy's cry, she slowly turned her head back toward him.

"Were you speaking to me?" she asked innocently.

D.J. cut his eyes sharply to the side without moving his head. Mrs. Higgins had turned around and was looking at him and her daughter. D.J. hesitated, knowing that nobody had seen Pris throwing the ice. He felt foolish as several people turned to stare at him and the girl. D.J. knew it looked to everyone as though he was being very unfair to Pris.

A little laugh behind him made the boy turn around, though it was always risky to turn his back on Pris. But she wouldn't do anything while people were watching.

"Somebody picking on you, D.J.?" Kathy Stagg asked teasingly, shaking her reddish-colored hair away from her blue eyes.

"It's OK."

For a moment, Kathy seemed about to say something else, for a teasing light remained in her eyes. Then her eyes grew serious. "You about ready for school?"

"I'm as ready as I'll ever be."

"I can hardly wait," Kathy said, sitting down on the end of a bench attached to a picnic table. "For the first time in my life, I'm hoping Dad won't move before the school year is over."

"That's good," he said.

"You going to bring your cub and dog to school with you?" Her blue eyes lit up again and he knew she was teasing him. He didn't like it.

"On special occasions, sure."

"I'm surprised you didn't bring them to the picnic."

D.J. didn't know what to say. He just wished she'd go away and leave him alone, and yet he liked seeing her too. It was something he couldn't explain.

"I hear the cub's growing like a summer weed."

"Gaining maybe 10 pounds a month, I'd guess. Going to be a big one next spring when the movie people come around."

"You're still counting on that?"

"Aren't you?"

Kathy looked thoughtful. "It'll be interesting to see how a movie is made. Of course, I'd like to have a small part in that film, but there's no way of knowing if that'll happen. The Chamber of Commerce at Indian Springs is going to help line up extras, and everybody around here will want a part."

"Your father can help you get a part, can't he?"

"He's just a contact man. He has nothing to do with who gets hired for a part."

"Well, I'm expecting to get a part with Koko. In fact, Alfred and I taught the cub to walk on his hind legs like a person, carry a small American flag on a staff in his left paw over his shoulder, and salute with his right forepaw."

The boy felt proud of that trick and expected Kathy to be impressed. Instead, she frowned and didn't answer.

D.J. added, "When Koko and I are in that movie, people all over the world will see us and know I've got a pet bear."

Kathy stood up. "You're not going to keep that bear until spring, are you?"

"Going to keep him forever!"

Kathy said, "When I asked you to help trap Ol' Satchel Foot alive so his sore jaw could be treated and then he could be released in the high country to live out his natural life, you did it."

"Didn't do it for *you*," he said weakly. "Did it because it was a good thing for that old outlaw."

"Then don't you think it's a good idea to do the same thing for that cub?"

"Turn him *loose?* He'd starve! In fact, he'd have

died back there when he was a little fellow if I
hadn't saved him."

"How do you know he won't survive if he's returned to the wilds? After all, he's a wild animal
and you've taken him from his natural grounds to
raise him like a dog or a cat."

D.J. felt himself getting annoyed. "Koko loves the
city! He loves to come to town! He likes being
around people, and when I take him for a walk in
the woods, he can hardly wait to get home."

"A regular city bear, is he?"

"Now that you mention it—yes, he is!"

Suddenly loud voices stopped the discussion before it got any warmer. D.J. recognized Dad's angry
tones even before the boy saw a curious crowd
closing a circle around Dad and someone D.J.
couldn't see. But D.J. knew who it was even before
Kathy exclaimed, "That's my father's voice." She
ran off.

D.J. raced past her and pushed his way through
the circle of picnickers. Dad had thrown his hat
onto the ground in front of Paul Stagg. Dad stood
with his left leg forward, his left fist up, and his
right fist drawn back. The pastor's open hands
were up, palms facing Dad, trying to calm him. D.J.
felt sick inside. Dad was always getting into fights
and arguments, even against a man who stood
more than head and shoulders above him.

Mrs. Stagg pushed through the crowd the same
moment D.J. and Kathy got there. Mrs. Stagg
rushed up to her husband asking, "Paul, what on
earth. . . ?"

The big man used his right hand to gently push

her behind him, but his eyes didn't leave Sam Dillon's angry face. "Now, Sam, let's let these good people go on with their picnic and you and I'll go sit in the car and talk like gentlemen."

Dad yelled, "We'll do NO such thing! I thought you were a bear hunter and a hound dog man, so I liked you! But then you got to meddling in MY business, and I don't like it! Not one bit!"

"Sam, I know you don't believe me, but I don't have any idea of what you're talking about!"

"I'm talking about turning this town into a place where everybody's getting religion!"

Paul tried to smile gently. "If you mean that I'm trying to lead people to the Lord and help them have the kind of life He wanted, then I'm guilty."

"Well, watch who you're filling with those ideas!"

D.J. wanted to interfere, but he had only done that once. Dad had backhanded him and then jumped on the other man before the sheriff's deputies arrived. It had taken six of them to get Dad into the patrol car.

"Sam, I think I know who you mean, but let's not discuss it here. Why don't we step over someplace where we can have a little quiet."

A child's scream broke into Paul's sentence. Everyone turned back toward the sound. Through the hole that opened in the crowd, D.J. saw a little girl about five years old standing on top of a picnic table. She was shrieking hysterically, an empty ice cream cone gripped in both hands. The scoop of ice cream lay on the attached redwood bench. A cinnamon-colored young bear was enthusiastically licking the ice cream.

"KOKO!"

D.J. raced across the grass followed by a screaming woman he guessed was the child's mother. The boy grabbed the broken chain and pulled the cub firmly away from the last signs of the ice cream. Koko bounced playfully against D.J.'s legs, smearing ice cream on his clean pants. The woman picked up her child, quieted her, and then turned to D.J.

"You ought to be ashamed!" she cried. "That beast could have killed my girl!"

"Look, ma'am, he broke his chain. See? And he wouldn't hurt anybody! He's just a cub who loves people. Look how he's playing with my shoe!"

"He's trying to eat your foot off! I'm going to have the law on you! Where's a deputy? Anybody seen a deputy?" The woman turned away, angrily pushing her way through the crowd, holding her daughter in her arms.

"Come on, Koko!" D.J. whispered, bending to pick up the cub. He was getting to be quite an armful. "Let's get out of here until things calm down."

The boy ran across the park, ducking behind some junipers that hid him from view. D.J. ran until he couldn't hear anybody following him. Then he sank down behind a memorial monument.

"Oh, Koko, what'm I going to do with you? Dad said I'd have to get rid of you if you got into mischief! Now look what you've done!"

Suddenly, angry shouts and screams erupted from back at the picnic. "Oh! Oh!" D.J. cried. "Trouble!"

Chapter Seven

SECRET THREAT TO THE CUB

D.J. ran back to the picnic as fast as Koko could follow. The boy saw the circle of townspeople and knew, from the angry voice of his father, who was in the center of that ring. D.J. pushed his way through the crowd. Most dropped back automatically when they saw the cub. D.J. groaned when he reached the inner circle.

He thought, *Oh, no! Why does my father have to always be mad at everybody? Lord, why can't You touch his heart and change him?*

A uniformed deputy sheriff was standing between Sam Dillon and Paul Stagg. The deputy held his black baton in his right hand, the end resting lightly in his left. "Now, Mr. Dillon, I'm only going to say this one more time: go home quietly—now!"

D.J. rushed up and grabbed his father's shirt sleeve. The boy whispered, "Let's go home, Dad. Please?"

For a moment, his dad hesitated. Then he said softly to the deputy, "Can I have a minute with Hannah Higgins?"

The officer knew everyone in the small community. He turned to look at the widow. She bit her lower lip thoughtfully, then nodded briefly. The deputy stepped aside and raised his voice, "All right, folks. Go back to your picnic. Give these people a little privacy."

The people moved away as Dad glowered at Paul Stagg. Dad walked over to Mrs. Higgins, who bent and spoke softly to her daughter. Pris moved back uncertainly. D.J. stood where he was, keeping the cub's chain short so the bear was forced against the boy's knee.

Paul Stagg bent over. "D.J., I'm powerful sorry about all this."

"It's not your fault. Dad always fights with everybody. He's been worse lately."

The big man sat down on a redwood picnic bench and motioned the boy to sit beside him. D.J. glanced at his father. He was talking quietly to Mrs. Higgins while the deputy stood nearby. D.J. asked, "Why can't my dad be like other fathers? Like Alfred's, for instance?"

"I can't rightly answer that, D.J. A child's world should be fun, with people who're always nice. But in the real world, kids sometimes get parents who drink, beat their wives or children, and do other terrible things. That's the way it is, but I take comfort in the thought that it'll somehow come out all right, especially for us believers. Do you know Romans 8:28?"

The boy shook his head. The lay pastor reached into the right hip pocket of his blue jeans and produced a well-used pocket New Testament. He thumbed to the passage with obvious ease.

"It's one of the most comforting verses in the Bible," Paul Stagg rumbled in his deep bass voice. "The Apostle Paul wrote, 'And we know that God causes all things to work together for good to those who love God, to those who are called according to His purpose.' "

The boy thought about that. "I love God; at least, I try. But Dad's getting worse and he makes me — well, ashamed and sorry and all kinds of things."

"Of course you love the Lord, D.J.! And remember Jesus changed your grandfather. The Lord can change your father too."

"That's what Mom used to say, but I don't see it happening."

"We've got to keep praying and believing."

The boy absently reached down and scratched the cub's chest. Koko lay down on his back and raised his feet in the air. He closed his eyes and seemed to be really enjoying the boy's gentle scratching.

"Maybe it's the second part of that verse where I'm messing up," the boy mused. "I mean, where it says 'to those who are called according to His purpose.' "

"Do you doubt you're called 'according to His purpose,' D.J.?"

"I don't know *what* my purpose is, except to someday write books and things. But I'm probably supposed to be doing something right now and I'm not doing it. So it's probably my fault."

"What is?" the big man rumbled.

The boy hesitated before answering. Except for Alfred and Grandpa, D.J. hadn't told anyone about his being afraid to witness to Dad. "Well," D.J. said with a little sigh, "I know I should tell everyone about giving my life to Jesus. But I'm afraid of what Dad would say or do, and so I haven't said anything except to Grandpa. We read the Bible together, but only when Dad's not around."

"And you're feeling guilty?"

The boy nodded. He stopped scratching the cub. Koko opened his eyes and reached up to push his nose against the boy's hand. D.J.'s fingers moved again.

"I guess so. A lot."

"Believers shouldn't feel guilty. You should ask the Lord to forgive you for not speaking up as His witness. Then pray the Lord will give you the courage to be a good witness to your father and anybody else."

D.J. thought of Nails Abst. D.J. could already imagine the jeers and laughter if he told Nails about the commitment he had made.

The boy swallowed hard and glanced at his father. Dad was still talking to Mrs. Higgins. She was facing D.J., but looking up at Sam Dillon's face. Dad's voice was so low the boy couldn't hear what he was saying. That meant Dad's anger was probably gone. The boy lowered his head as the big preacher's deep voice began a fervent prayer about D.J.'s problem.

When Paul finished, D.J. opened his eyes. Dad was standing beside him. Instinctively, the boy stepped back, half-expecting his father to smack him. Instead, Dad asked, "You too, D.J.?"

For a moment, the boy hesitated, fighting the fear that surged through his body. Then he nodded. "I gave my life to Jesus when Ol' Satchel Foot was climbing that tree after me. But I've been afraid to tell you."

Dad was surprisingly calm. D.J. saw Mrs. Higgins was standing where Dad had left her. The deputy was also close by. Dad said softly, "I don't want you to be afraid of me, Son. I want you to love me."

D.J. looked up and thought he saw tears in his father's eyes. D.J. dropped the cub's chain and threw his arms around his father's waist. The boy laid his head against Dad's powerful chest.

"O Dad! I do love you!"

For a moment, the man's arms circled out and stopped in midair. Then they slowly closed about the boy. Dad didn't say anything more, but he squeezed so hard the boy thought every one of his ribs would be broken.

Dad finally spoke. His voice was trembly. "Paul, I'm sorry."

The big man's voice rumbled up from deep in his chest. "No apology necessary, Sam."

"Thanks," Dad said. "Let's go home, Son."

On the drive into the country, D.J. stared out the pickup window, thinking. Dad had twice called him "Son." Dad had hugged him. He had done that right after the boy had confessed giving his life to the Lord. That was exactly 100 percent different from what D.J. had expected. Maybe the tall lay preacher was right, and God did make all things work together for good. But D.J. still had to tell Nails Abst. He cringed, imagining the older boy's laughing, jeering reaction. D.J. wasn't ready to do that yet.

Dad eased the pickup off the paved county road and gently entered the creek below the house. "I've been wanting to talk to you about something, D.J."

The boy looked up at his father. His face was softer than D.J. had seen it in a long time. Usually Dad's face was dark with anger.

"I've been thinking about getting married. I need to know how you feel, Son."

D.J. swallowed hard, but he didn't say anything. The pain of having another woman act as his mother hurt too much. It was worse because of Priscilla.

Dad spoke again, shifting the pickup into second gear as the rear wheels cleared the creek and the climb up the hill began. "It may not happen because Hannah says she won't marry me unless I become a Christian too."

D.J. still didn't say anything. He rubbed his shoe sole gently against the cub which rested on the floorboards. Dad spoke again.

"Hannah told me today the same thing she did the night I took you with me when we first heard about the possible strike. She says I can't change through will-power alone, or if I did, it'd only be for a while. She says I've got to be cleaned up completely, and no man can do that for himself. She wanted me to start going to church, but I won't do that."

D.J. wanted to ask why not, but he kept quiet.

His father continued, "I blamed the preacher for her talking like that. But Hannah says he has nothing to do with it. It's her decision. I guess she's right, though I thought I'd feel better if I hit that big horse a couple of solid licks."

The boy knew from long experience that he could get smacked in the mouth next if he said anything his father didn't like, but D.J. had to say it. "Paul Stagg's a mighty nice person."

Dad looked down at his son and nodded. "I know. But that still doesn't make me feel any better. And I don't know that I can ever change. But if I could, and Hannah married me, how would you feel?"

The boy licked his lips before answering. "I wouldn't like it much," he said softly.

Dad nodded, but didn't say anything. He shifted gears again and drove in silence up to the house.

Grandpa was rocking on the front porch. He hadn't been feeling well that morning, so he had stayed home from the picnic. D.J. watched the old red rocker's gentle, even movements. Grandpa was learning not to get mad when he was left alone or things bothered him.

Dad spoke again as he and D.J. climbed down from the pickup. "We don't need those hounds anymore. I'm taking them all to Boot Malloy and trade them off."

Sudden fear speared the boy's heart. "Not Hero!"

Dad shook his head. "Not your mutt," he said.

D.J. led the cub by the broken chain toward the house, feeling such relief the boy's heart seemed about to fly off like a kite in a March wind.

Dad walked beside him. "We'll say no more about marrying."

* * * * *

The next day, D.J. rode with his father to the trader's ramshackle place to trade the hounds. Boot Malloy's innocent brown eyes roamed over the bear-hunting dogs he'd sold to Dad some months before.

"I dunno, Sam," Boot began, squatting on his boot heels in the dust by his old red barn. "You must'a run them there hounds powerful hard."

Dad's voice instantly showed his hair-trigger temper. "Why, you ornery old reprobate! You know I didn't run them hounds half as hard as the guy who sold them to you before you swapped 'em to me! You're just trying to squeeze me out of a fair deal!"

D.J. slowly sucked in his breath. Mrs. Higgins was right. Dad couldn't change himself. He was still contrary and mean tempered inside.

Boot Malloy took a plug of chewing tobacco from the hip pocket of his bib overalls. "Chaw?" he asked Dad.

"Don't go trying to change the subject on me, Boot Malloy!"

"Just being sociable, Sam! Just being sociable! Well, tell you what: you throw in that there bear cub and I just might make you a real good deal."

D.J. had been leaning in the shade of the barn, but the words brought him up to his feet. "Koko's *not* for sale! And neither is my hair-pulling bear dog!"

"Make you a powerful good trade, D.J."

The boy shook his head. "No, thanks."

Dad finally traded the hounds off, including the pups that Koko had slept with when he had first been captured. On the drive back home, D.J. asked, "Dad, why do you suppose Boot Malloy tried so hard to get me to give up this cub?"

"Don't rightly know, but you can be sure that sharp old coot of a trader knows something nobody else does. Seems it has something to do with that bear. Now, if I was you, I'd keep a sharp eye on that there cub of yours."

The words cut through D.J.'s insides like a buzz saw through pine. "You don't think he'd do anything to Koko?"

"Wouldn't harm the cub, that's for sure. There'd be no money in that. So Boot Malloy's got something else up his sleeve."

"Like what?"

"Hard to say, but it means money to him. The way he tried to swap for your cub shows somebody wants him mighty bad."

"You mean like Nails Abst?"

"Don't think so. That kid is just a bully, and he'll bluster and threaten and take from them who're littler than he is. No, I'd guess Boot has an adult in mind who's looking for a cub."

"Maybe the movie people who're coming to shoot that picture next spring?"

"They got their own bear. Besides, they'd always get new ones from regular suppliers in Southern California. No, D.J., there's somebody else around who wants a bear cub, and the way Boot acted, the price is right. Somebody wants a pet bear mighty bad. You watch out for yours."

"I will!" D.J. exclaimed, feeling the hot fear race through his blood. "I will!"

School would start the next week, and both Koko and Hero would be home alone except for Grandpa. Suddenly, D.J. was very afraid of what might happen to his little cub while he was at school.

AN OPPORTUNITY AND A MYSTERY

D.J. didn't see Alfred until the day school started. D.J. got on the bob-tailed yellow bus designed for the short, tight mountain curves that led to Stoney Ridge Grammar School. D.J. greeted the driver, Mrs. Schmidt, and then all the friends he hadn't seen since last June. Almost everyone had heard about D.J.'s experiences in capturing the outlaw bear and about the cub. D.J. tried to answer questions by raising his voice above the noisy bus, but everyone was talking at once.

Several other students were waiting at the bus stop where Alfred got on. He hung back, his thick eyeglasses reflecting the morning sun. D.J. called out the window and Alfred waved and smiled. He got on last and at once everyone started saying things about the new boy and his thick glasses. D.J. had held an aisle seat for Alfred. He sat down quickly and slumped down so he was almost out of

sight between the high-backed seats. D.J. understood the shy newcomer was trying to make himself invisible.

D.J. said, "Hey, Alfred, it's OK! They're my friends
from school! They always pick on a new kid at first!"

Alfred whispered, "Do you hear what they're saying? I can't help having to wear these dumb ol'
glasses!"

"I've got an idea, Alfred." D.J. sat up straight and
cupped his hands to his mouth. "Hey, everybody,
this is Alfred. He helps me train my bear cub."

Instantly, the noisy students' remarks turned into
excited comments. That relationship with the cub
made Alfred special, and he quickly acted on it. He
raised his head slightly. His eyes darted around the
bus. Alfred sat up straight. "I know all about
bears," he announced timidly.

It was a challenge that brought only silence for a
moment. Then someone yelled from the back of
the bus, "Prove it!"

"OK," Alfred said, "I will." He sat up very tall in
the seat and raised his voice. "The California black
bear—which Koko is—is omnivorous in feeding
habits—"

"Omnee what?" a seventh-grader named Dale
Masters interrupted.

"Means he'll eat almost anything," Alfred explained. "That includes berries, insects, vegetation,
frogs, fruit, nuts, and carrion."

Dale yelled, "What's that?"

Mary Antoli, a sixth-grader, made a face and
called, "Dead things!"

The bus load of students wanted to know more

about bears and especially the cub, but D.J. was anxious to talk about what Boot Malloy had said. He lowered his voice so only Alfred could hear. "I've got to talk to you."

"What about?"

D.J. leaned closer to whisper in Alfred's right ear. "About somebody who wants to get ahold of Koko *real* bad."

"You mean Nails Abst?"

"Don't think so." D.J. ignored the students still wanting to know about bears. D.J. explained about the trip to Boot Malloy's, and what Dad had said.

When D.J. had finished, Alfred pushed his heavy glasses farther up on his nose. "Good! We've got a mystery on our hands, haven't we?"

"All I know is that I'm scared of what might happen to Koko when I'm at school."

"If somebody did steal him, we could use your dog to find him."

D.J. sat up and grinned. "We could, couldn't we?"

Alfred frowned thoughtfully. "Well, maybe we could and maybe we couldn't. Let's make sure by training Hero to trail and find Koko. Something like hide and seek, only with animals instead of kids. I'll help, of course."

"That's a good idea, Alfred! Oh! Oh! The next stop is where Nails Abst gets on!"

The little bus growled around a curve and pulled off next to a small bus shelter big enough for half a dozen students. But this year there was only one student—Nails. He looked much older than everyone else. D.J. guessed that was because Nails had failed a couple of grades. Nails got up slowly from the bench inside the shelter and unhurriedly walked toward the bus, kicking at pebbles and dirt clods.

The lady bus driver, Mrs. Schmidt, held the door open and called, "Hurry up!"

Nails didn't reply, but he didn't hurry either. He raised his eyes and glowered at every window. His lips seemed to curl into a sneer, then his eyes brightened when he caught D.J.'s blue eyes. Nails immediately jumped into the bus so fast Mrs. Schmidt warned him not to do that again.

Nails pushed his way back to where Alfred was sitting on the aisle with D.J. by the window. "Well, now, look who's here! My two most favorite enemies, Alfred the Owl and D.J. the Cub Boy!"

D.J. said, "Don't call names!"

"Who's going to stop me?"

The driver looked into the big rearview mirror and told Nails to sit down. He muttered something under his breath and started toward the back of the bus.

Alfred sighed. "It's going to be a long school year, D.J."

D.J. didn't say anything, but he thought that might be the truth. And it wasn't going to be easy to tell Nails that he was now a Christian. D.J. looked out the window. The sun was shining and the hills were beautiful, but suddenly D.J. felt winter closing in on his heart.

The bus pulled up a small hill that led directly into the higher mountains. The bus door swung open. Yelling students piled out onto the concrete sidewalk in front of the small white frame school. D.J. motioned for Alfred to stay seated until every-

one else was off the bus. Nails was the last one to
move up the aisle. He stopped and looked down at
the two boys.

"I'm going to have my bear, D.J. Dillon!"

"It's *not* your bear!"

"Will be soon, or it'll be nobody's bear."

Nails grinned without humor and went on to the
front of the bus and out onto the school grounds.
D.J. and Alfred exchanged glances.

Alfred said worriedly, "That sounded like a
threat, didn't it?"

"He's just talking to hear himself talk," D.J. said
with forced cheerfulness. "Let me show you where
everything is."

D.J. explained that classes for all eight grades
were held here. The school had been built at the
eastern end of town because land was cheaper and
the town was expected to grow that way. The
school playground was next to an old cemetery. On
the other side of the school yard to the right, past
the bus sheds, there was an open field. Beyond
that, evergreen trees followed the series of ridges
and hills that finally soared so high snow would not
melt until late May each year.

Kathy Stagg came running up, her reddish-colored hair bouncing. Behind her, Pris Higgins also
trotted up. The older girl's blue eyes were bright
with excitement.

"Guess what?" she said, then plunged ahead
without waiting for an answer. "Jay Calkins — Daddy's friend from the movie company — is back in
town and he wants to see you."

"Me?" D.J. asked. "How come?"

Kathy shrugged. "He didn't say. But Daddy's going to bring him over at noon so you can talk."

Pris exclaimed, "And he's going to speak at assembly this week! My teacher, Miss Franzen, already told me so."

D.J. usually liked school, but today he couldn't keep his mind on things. D.J. found himself looking out the windows toward the street. When the noon bell rang, he hurried outside and stood at the bus stop by the curb. He saw Alfred, Kathy, and Pris coming toward him from different directions.

The boy recognized Paul Stagg's old sedan as it turned the corner and pulled up alongside. D.J. saw the movie man's smiling face at the passenger's side window.

"Hello, D.J.! Good to see you again! Hop in!"

"Hi, Mr. Calkins! Hello, Paul," the boy replied, leaning over to shake the movie man's extended hand. "Can't leave the school grounds."

Paul Stagg leaned across the front seat and grinned up at the boy. "I should have remembered that. Well, then let's get out and talk on the lawn."

Kathy, Pris, and Alfred arrived a little out of breath to find out what was going on. D.J. felt a little bothered by the girls. He didn't mind having Alfred around though.

Mr. Calkins stood on the lawn and turned slowly in a complete circle. "Beautiful country around here! Beautiful! Make a great background for the series we're going to shoot."

"Series?" Kathy asked. "I thought you were just going to make one picture?"

"We were! We were! But our research has shown

that a series with mountains and bears would be profitable."

At the mention of bears, D.J.'s heart jumped. So that's what Boot Malloy must have known was going to happen!

Mr. Calkins' continued. "We've learned that people like certain things in their Quality Family Productions. They love summer and outdoor mountain scenes, and they like certain animals, but not others."

Alfred nodded, the sun reflecting off his thick glasses. "Boys like dogs, girls like horses, and everybody—including grown-ups—likes bears."

Mr. Calkins slapped Alfred on the back so hard his glasses slipped off one ear. The boy grabbed for them and pushed them back as the movie man explained. "That's right! Maybe that's because bears can walk upright like a man and do things with their forepaws, such as holding things. Anyway, people *love* bears. So that's why I'm here. D.J., how would you like to sell us your cub?"

The words came as a hard crack on the back of the neck with a big stick. D.J. opened his mouth, but no words came. Alfred didn't have any trouble speaking up.

"Koko's *not* for sale!"

Paul Stagg chuckled, the sound rumbling up from his big chest like a distant mountain rock slide. "Well, now, Alfred! You seem pretty certain about what D.J.'s going to say!"

Alfred's shyness returned. He lowered his head and didn't say anything more. Pris clapped her hands and jumped about. "Oh, goody! Koko's going to be a movie star!"

Kathy frowned and said, "No wild animal should be kept in captivity! That bear cub should be—"

D.J. interrupted. "Alfred's right. I won't sell my cub."

Mr. Calkins pursed his lips. "I was afraid you might say that. All right, let me ask you a question. Does your bear do tricks?"

D.J. exclaimed, "I'll say! Why, Koko can do all sorts of tricks and I can teach him more!"

Alfred said, "I'll help!"

Mr. Calkins grinned. "That's great! Of course, this business is unpredictable, and the producer might not be able to use any of those tricks. However, it might be worth more money to the producer for him to know the cub can do such things. So I'd suggest you go ahead and do all you can so you're ready when we come here to do the 'shoot' next spring. What do you say?"

D.J. nodded. "Sounds fine to me, but I can't promise you what my father will say, Mr. Calkins."

"I understand! I understand! Just remember, we need a young bear that can be trained and ready by next May. You could make enough to put yourself through college if we make a deal."

Pris squealed with delight and clapped her hands, but Kathy just shook her head in disapproval. Alfred beamed and patted D.J. on the shoulder.

D.J. asked, "If we don't make a deal, Mr. Calkins, what then?"

"Then I'll have to find another bear. That's why I've got to move so quickly. And it's only fair to tell you I've heard about someone else in this area who has a bear cub for me to check out."

D.J. frowned. "Another cub around here?"

"That's what I've heard, my boy! Well, I've got to run. See you later."

As the two men drove off, D.J. looked after them with a deep frown. "Alfred, nobody else around here has a cub or we'd have heard about it, right?"

"Exactly!" Alfred said firmly. "So that means somebody's been expecting to get our bear and claim it for their own!"

"But they can't do that!" D.J. protested.

"Logically, no," Alfred said, adjusting his glasses. "But we'd better not turn our backs on Koko for a minute or he may be gone!"

"Even if they did kidnap Koko, we'd recognize him! They couldn't get away with that!"

Kathy's blue eyes crackled with annoyance. "You're both overlooking something! Suppose there *is* another bear cub around? If anything happened to your bear, then that other cub would get the movie part."

Pris asked, "What could happen to Koko?"

Alfred turned his owlish eyes upon her. "He could get kidnapped or killed, that's what!"

D.J. cried, "No! Alfred, don't say that!"

Alfred looked up at his friend and said quietly, "You know it's true, D.J."

For a moment, the mountain boy did not speak. Then slowly he nodded, feeling his insides get cold and heavy. Koko was in real danger, and would be for the next eight months!

Chapter Nine

THE CUB DISAPPEARS

That night D.J. got off the school bus and removed his shoes to wade the creek. He was surprised that Grandpa wasn't sitting on the porch. Then D.J. remembered that his grandfather hadn't been feeling well. The boy ran on up the hill, a tightness settling upon his chest. Hero dashed out from under the porch and barked sharply. He stood on his hind legs and pawed the air, whining to reach the boy.

D.J. reached down and patted the little hair-puller."Hello, Hero! How's the dog, huh? That's good! You been taking good care of the cub? OK, that's enough petting for a while. I've got to see Koko now."

The boy went on past the porch toward the dog-house where Koko had slept with the pups last summer. D.J. called, "Hey, Koko! I'm home!" There was no answering rattle of chain from the bear. Suddenly, D.J. stopped dead still.

The afternoon sun glinted on the cub's chain. It lay like a silver necklace in the dust outside the doghouse. But the bear was not in sight.

"Oh, no!" D.J. moaned. "Not again!" Quickly the boy bent and looked inside the doghouse. It was empty. D.J. ran around the house, calling, "Koko! Here, Koko!" in the same manner he'd call the dog. He heard the pigs grunting and crashing against their feeding trough. A hummingbird hovered over one of Grandpa's roses blooming behind the single strand of electric fence. A light breeze, hinting of coming autumn, whispered among the tops of the evergreen trees. A redheaded woodpecker drummed on a ghostly gray dead tree trunk, hammering an acorn in for the winter. But there was no sound from the bear cub.

D.J. dashed inside the house and into Grandpa's bedroom. He slept in the front one nearest the porch and off the dining-living room. The old man was sitting up in bed, reading the Bible that had belonged to D.J.'s mother.

"Grandpa, where's Koko?"

The old man lowered his Bible and looked over the top of his wire-rimmed bifocals. "Isn't he chained up where he belongs?"

"No! His chain's there, but he's gone. Must've broken the chain at his collar. I'd better go look for him. I'll take Hero along. OK?"

Grandpa hesitated a moment, then managed a weak smile. "You run along, D.J. And don't worry! You'll find him before supper!"

But D.J. didn't find the cub. He found the bear's tracks leading away from the house. In the thick dust, the front paw print was clear. It was small and almost round. The hind paw was much longer, shaped more like a man's, except there was no raised part where a human arch would have been. Bears walk flat-footed, D.J. knew. The whole foot showed, from the wide front claws to the narrow rounded heel. But instead of having a big toe on the inside, as a human does, the bear's two middle toes were almost even in length. They stuck well out in front so the longest toes showed in the middle.

"Here, Hero," D.J. called to the little mixed-breed mutt. "Stick your nose down here and get Koko's scent. Then follow him. Go on! Find Koko!" D.J. gently pushed the little hair-puller's long black nose into the bear tracks. When the dog sniffed and noisily blew dust out of his nostrils with a lot of sneezes, the boy waved his arm in the direction the paw marks led. "Go on! Find Koko!"

Hero barked sharply, hurting the boy's ears. The little dog dashed off, eager to please. However, the little mutt didn't really understand what was expected. He thought D.J. wanted to play, as they often did. The hair-puller ran in a wide circle, scaring up some mountain quail. They exploded like shotgun shells and whirred off like winged bullets, scattering in all directions.

The dog barked happily at them and then circled back to D.J., trailing sharp, loud barks with every step. The mutt ran with his stub tail tucked tightly against his body. His hindquarters were drawn so far up under him that Hero seemed to almost be sitting down while dashing around like a dust devil.

The boy laughed in spite of himself. "Oh, Hero!

You're a sight! But you're as useless as notching a stick! Well, when we find Koko, I'm going to take Alfred's suggestion and teach you to trail and find that cub. Now, let's see if we can find him before dark."

Dusk settled so fast over the hills it was like a blanket dropped from a giant's hands. The boy and dog returned to the house. As D.J. entered the screened kitchen door after chaining Hero outside, Dad looked up from where he was making dinner. "The chores aren't done!" he roared, his face starting to turn dark with anger.

"I know," D.J. said lamely. "Koko's gone. I've been looking for him."

"Your grandfather told me. He's feeling kinda puny and you should be here with him! Instead, you're out looking for that fool bear! Now you get those chores done and then we'll have a little set-to,* young man!"

The boy was too concerned about Koko to worry about what his father might say or do. D.J. fed the hogs without even thinking of what he was doing. He split live oak and madrona by the light of the back porch's hundred-watt bulb. He carried armloads of the dry hardwood into the kitchen for the wood-burning stove. Dad was making pancakes for supper. They smelled so good D.J.'s tongue flickered over his lips in anticipation of tasting them, but he knew better than to stop to eat just yet. He carried the trash out and dumped it in a far corner where eventually it would be trucked away to the county dump. D.J. fed Hero, patted him, and then walked inside to wash his hands in the kitchen sink.

"Grandpa's not getting up for supper?" the boy

asked, drying his hands on an old flour sack that hung by the sink.

"I told you he's feeling under the weather!" Dad's voice was sharp. He finished pouring homemade apple butter over the last half pancake and ate it. "You'd think you'd be more interested in your own flesh and blood than in a bear!"

D.J. walked across the kitchen linoleum, and crossed the second faded print linoleum in the combination dining room and living room, and into Grandpa's bedroom. The old man was dozing, his bifocals well down on his nose, his gray hair covering his bald spot. The open Bible lay on his knees. The Irish shillelagh Grandpa used as a cane lay beside his thin, brown-blotched right hand.

For a moment, the boy hesitated. He was suddenly aware just how weak and frail Grandpa looked. The old man's pale blue eyes blinked open and he smiled weakly.

"That you, D.J.?"

"Yes, Grandpa. Can't you see me?"

"Guess my eyes are getting worse. Dag-nabbed glasses ain't worth the powder to blow them up! Still, it beats being blind, I guess. Did you find your bear?"

"Not yet."

Grandpa patted the bed with his left hand. "Sit down here a minute. I want to talk to you."

The boy sat, noticing up close how Grandpa's jaws were sinking in deeply. D.J. thought Grandpa had forgotten to put in his false teeth, but a glance at the water glass on the old pine nightstand showed the dentures were not there. He was wearing them, but his cheeks were very sunken.

"D.J., I hear you finally told your father about your commitment to the Lord."

"Yes, I did."

"How'd he take it?"

"Fine. Surprised me."

"I'm glad. Boy or man shouldn't have to feel ashamed of saying what he believes, even if it does mean somebody's not going to like it."

"I'm not ashamed, Grandpa; I just couldn't say it right off."

"Well, no matter; guess that's kind of like spiritual growth I hear tell about. Kinda like that there bear cub of yours; lots of growth, day by day. Sometimes so little you don't notice it, but suddenly one day you look and say, 'My! That cub has growed considerable!' Same with spiritual things, I guess. I've been trying to grow too."

The boy didn't know what to say. He waited, feeling Grandpa was about to mention something important. The old man took D.J.'s hand in both of his.

"D.J., you know why I went forward in church some time back and gave my heart to the Lord after all these years of living my own way?"

"Because you wanted to?"

The old man chuckled and went into a coughing spell. His face turned red and D.J. jumped up in alarm. He didn't know what to do and so just waited until the coughing passed. Grandpa sighed and rubbed his teary eyes with the back of a thin hand.

"Guess time is slipping by faster'n I dreamt, D.J.! Whew! Each time gets worse, it seems."

The boy frowned. He hadn't thought about hearing Grandpa cough, but he had been doing it a lot lately, D.J. realized. "You'll be OK," he said, taking the old man's left hand in his.

"Getting close to checkout time in this old hotel," Grandpa said, tapping his bony chest with his free right hand.

D.J. exclaimed, "Don't talk like that!"

"Got to happen, sooner or later. Well, as I was saying, I went forward and recommitted my life to the Lord because I really wanted to. 'Course, there's some in this town would say I was just a'getting fire insurance, but that's not true! I don't mind keeping away from down below, you understand, but when I sleep on the hill near your mother, I don't want you to think—"

"Grandpa!" D.J. jumped up and dropped the old hand. "I don't want you to talk like that! You're going to get well!"

The old man smiled and D.J. thought he saw the watery blue eyes glisten with tears. "Tell you what, D.J. I'd like to stick around and see you graduate from eighth grade."

The boy slowly let out a breath of air he hadn't even realized he was holding in. "Good! Then you can also see my bear in the movies! A whole bunch of movies in a series if I want."

"Nothing would please me more. But there's something else you should know so you can't hold me to anything if I don't stick around for spring."

A cold wind seemed to whip up around D.J.'s heart. He swallowed hard and asked quietly, "What's that, Grandpa?"

"There comes a time when you've got to gather up your memories—that way nothing's really lost—and then you go on. That's the way things are: you gather for a while, then you finally have to let go and move on, taking only the memories."

D.J. frowned and started to say he didn't understand, but Dad's roar interrupted. The boy jumped up and raced into the kitchen. Dad had been in where the bathtub was. On returning to the kitchen, Dad had stopped stock-still. He was looking at the back screen door. It had been pushed aside at the bottom.

Dad yelled, "That bear must've done that! But where is he?"

D.J.'s heart sailed up like a buck deer springing happily across a meadow. The boy ran to the cupboard under the sink. The doors stood open. D.J. bent over and looked.

"KOKO! Where have you been? And what're you doing under there? You come out right now!"

He grabbed the cub's collar and pulled him backward into the light. The bear's muzzle was covered with apple butter. Dad exploded into a long string of cuss words, then suddenly began to laugh.

"Well, guess it's a cheap enough price to pay for not having to see you moping around all night, wondering where your cub was. But don't let it happen again, D.J.!"

"I'll get a heavier chain, Dad."

"You'd better! And while I think of it—Boot Malloy came by the mill this afternoon when I was picking up my check. Raised the price on that cub if you want to sell him."

"I won't sell him, Dad."

"That's what I told Boot, but he sure does want

that cub for some reason. If I was you, I'd keep a powerful close eye on him."

For the second time that day, D.J.'s fears gripped him in cold, icy fingers. "You don't think Boot would steal Koko?"

"No, he wouldn't. But whoever wants that bear is making it worthwhile for Boot to offer a mighty fancy figure for him. You be careful, or you won't have a cub one of these mornings."

"I'll be real careful. Oh, that reminds me, Dad. The movie man came to school today with Paul Stagg and offered to buy Koko."

"He did?"

"Yes," D.J. answered, and told him about the conversation. When he had finished, D.J. had cleaned up the apple butter and wiped off the cub's nose.

Dad rubbed a strong right hand across his stubble of fierce black whiskers. "Something mighty peculiar going on, D.J. You be careful."

"I will. Now I'd better see about fixing up a better chain for Koko."

"I'll whip up some fresh pancake batter for your supper when you finish."

The boy looked at his father a long time, surprised to see this gentler side to him. That was twice D.J. had been surprised, counting the time when Dad had hugged him at the Labor Day picnic. Maybe Mom had been right.

D.J. got the heaviest chain he could find and worked until well after 10 o'clock making the cub's collar stronger. "There," the boy said at last, leaning back and looking at the chain and collar, "that ought to hold you!"

He let the cub sleep on the foot of his bed as usual.
D.J. slid under the dusty-smelling covers and looked
up at the ceiling. He said his prayers, wondering if he
should get down on his knees. But the boy was
afraid Dad would laugh at him or maybe even cuss
him out. Dad was unpredictable that way. When
D.J. had finished praying for Grandpa's health,
Koko's safety, and a good year at school, the boy lay
awake awhile in the darkened house. He listened to
the coyotes and foxes yipping in the distance. Once
he thought he heard a mountain lion scream away
off toward Mad River.

Slowly, the boy's eyes closed and he began to drift
off. From a long way off, it seemed, he kept hearing
Grandpa's terrible coughing. It was getting worse.

Dad had changed his mind about D.J. having to
make Koko sleep outside. As long as D.J. kept Koko
out of trouble, the cub could sleep with D.J. Koko
made little sounds in his sleep, and the boy wondered if Koko was really in danger. The answer
made the boy suddenly sit upright in his rollaway
bed. He reached down and touched the growing
cub to be sure he was there.

"There's no doubt about it," D.J. thought as he
lay back down. "Somebody's out to get my cub! But
who? And why?"

No answer came, and D.J. finally slept. But it was
with an uneasy awareness that something strange
was going on.

Chapter Ten

A MOVIE CONTRACT AND A NEW PROBLEM

Over the next few weeks D.J. began to think his
fears were foolish. Only good things happened.
First, Nails Abst withdrew from school for a while
to help his father and their hounds chase a ridge-
running bear up in Siskiyou County. On his last day
of school at Stoney Ridge, Nails found D.J. and Alfred eating their sack lunches on the front lawn.

"Take good care of my cub while I'm gone,"
Nails said with a sneer. "I'll be back for him."

After Nails left, Alfred sighed and adjusted his
thick glasses with a forefinger. "D.J., I'm going to
sleep a lot easier now, knowing nothing's going to
happen to Koko."

D.J. finished chewing the last bite of his egg
sandwich before he answered. "I guess I should
too, but something bothers me."

"What's that?"

"Well, Nails has been threatening to take Koko

from me ever since I first got him. So why would Nails be the one who's had Boot Malloy trying to buy the cub from me?"

Alfred bit a chunk from an apple and chewed for a long time before answering. Finally he said, "I wish you hadn't said that, D.J."

But when nothing happened in the next few weeks, and Boot Malloy didn't make another offer, both boys began to rest easier. They were almost positive the Absts had been the ones trying to buy the cub.

Next, the mill settled its labor dispute without a strike, so Dad knew he'd not be out of work. D.J. was surprised to have Dad tell Grandpa that same evening, "Maybe I'll just go to church with D.J. next Sunday. Want to come along?"

"If I'm not still under the weather," the old man replied.

Grandpa wasn't feeling well on Sunday, but both D.J. and Dad dressed in their best. Instead of riding to Sunday School and church with a neighbor as he had been doing, D.J. climbed into Dad's pickup with him. Everyone at church welcomed Dad, especially Paul Stagg. Both men shook hands. Neither mentioned the scene at the Labor Day picnic. D.J. wasn't really sure why his father had suddenly decided to attend church, but the boy suspected it had something to do with Mrs. Higgins. When D.J. saw the widow and Dad talking by themselves after services, the boy felt he was right.

While the grown-ups were talking over coffee, D.J. told Alfred, "It's good that Dad went to church, but maybe he's doing it for the wrong reason. He's probably still thinking about marrying the widow."

"That bothers you a lot, doesn't it?" Alfred asked.

"Can't help it. I've told you often enough how I feel."

Later, when D.J. was resting on his rollaway bed with Koko at his feet, the boy wondered if Paul Stagg was right. Maybe, if all things *did* work together for good to those who love God, this could turn out OK. D.J. still didn't want Dad getting so friendly with Mrs. Higgins. Yet Dad was in a better mood lately, and maybe that was because of the widow.

*   *   *   *   *

D.J. and Alfred teamed up after school and on Saturdays to play a game of hide and seek with Koko and Hero. They wanted to see how good the hair-puller's half-hound bloodline would make Hero in trailing a bear. The air was turning cool so the scent stayed strong longer than in the hot summer. The boys took turns leading the bear out into the mountain wilderness.

After an hour's head start, the other boy released Hero and set him on the cub's trail. Since the cub and lead boy kept moving, sometimes it was getting dark before Hero threw up his head and bawled more like a hound than a dog barking. Whoever was following would cry, "Hero's winded* the bear!" and the race was on. Soon this was followed by a shout, "Now Hero's looking at him!"

Sure enough, the scruffy little mixed-breed mutt would lift his nose from the ground and cut across toward Koko. Following the scent in the air or off bushes where the cub had passed, Hero quickly found the hiding Koko and the other boy. Sometimes the chased boy and the cub would climb trees, forcing the dog to bay in frustration and jump repeatedly against the tree trunk. At other times, Koko chose to be "treed" on the ground. The cub backed up against a stump or log or boulder to protect his sensitive "tail feathers." The mutt jumped at the bear, barking steadily, then leaped away when Koko playfully struck at him. When Hero saw his chance, he raced around and leaped at Koko's hindquarters. The dog almost always playfully grabbed a mouthful of oily bear hair. Then Koko swatted at the dog or tried to sweep Hero up in his shaggy arms. Dog and bear rolled on the ground, growling and seeming to bite, but never hurting each other. D.J. and Alfred always ended up laughing hard at the mock ferociousness of the dog and cub tussles.

The game ended with the boys leading the tired, happy animals back to the Dillon house where Alfred's father picked him up and took him home.

In mid-October, D.J. told Alfred, "I'm going to start writing a story about us and those two." D.J. pointed at Hero and Koko with a pencil he'd started carrying on their hide-and-seek trips. "Maybe I'll sell the story to the movie people."

"Good idea!" Alfred said. "How about us starting with teaching Koko how to do some more new tricks he can use in the movie?"

"Well," D.J. said thoughtfully, "he can already do so many things. But when we take him to the scout meeting next month, let's see how many tricks he can do, both old and new."

*   *   *   *   *

At the scout meeting where D.J. had been invited to show the bear, Koko was doing great. He could walk upright like a man, drink from a soft-drink bottle held in his forepaws, roll over like a dog, play "dead," sit on his haunches and hold up his hind feet with his forepaws, wave to kids, or catch a thrown peanut in his mouth. Each time the bear did a trick, he was rewarded with one homemade biscuit smeared with strawberry jam. D.J. explained to the scouts that people thought bears liked honey most of all, but they liked strawberry jam or preserves better. Koko was really crazy about that sweet.

Alfred laughed often, saying, "The way that bear's putting on weight, he'll outweigh us both by springtime! Especially if we keep feeding him this stuff!"

One day a letter came from Mr. Calkins, the movie man. A contract from the producer was enclosed that required Dad's signature. D.J. could hardly wait for his father to get home from work to see if Dad would sign it. Dad carefully read the letter and the contract, then reread them. All the while, D.J. absently ran his finger over the raised letters and emblem on the envelope.

Finally Dad sucked in a deep breath and slowly let it out. "The letter says the movie people were not planning to shoot anything until spring so they could use outdoor scenes. Something about costing less when they didn't have to use artificial lights. But they've decided to shoot some outdoor scenes around Christmas so there'll be snow. And they'll take some pictures inside at an old warehouse they've rented over by the logging railroad."

D.J. was having a hard time keeping from dancing up and down because he'd already read that part

several times. But the boy knew better than to in-
terrupt Dad because then he probably would get
his "cussedness streak up" (as Grandpa had
warned the boy), and D.J. wouldn't get what he
wanted.

Dad went on, "They're offering you what they call
a 'walk-on' or 'bit' part in their movie, plus offering to
use your bear. You won't have a speaking part, but
they'll pay you for just walking on the set in a little
scene, and they'll pay for Koko to be with you."

It was all D.J. could do to keep from exclaiming,
"I know! I know!" But Dad wouldn't have liked that,
so the boy simply asked excitedly, "Can I, Dad? I
mean—can we? Koko and me? And maybe they'll
let Hero be in the movie too!"

Dad was in a rare good mood. He chuckled.
"Hold on now! Don't go getting selfish. Take the
part for yourself and the cub if you want, but don't
push for your dog unless they suggest that themselves. Fair enough?"

"I'll say!" D.J. exclaimed. He watched Dad carefully
sign the contract. D.J. could barely sleep that night.
The next morning, D.J. told everyone on the school
bus about the contract. When they got to school, D.J.
and Alfred told Kathy and Pris and just about everyone else. Everyone was excited except Kathy.

She said, "You know that's a wild animal and he
should be returned to the mountains."

"Don't you ever get tired of saying that?" D.J. demanded. "Koko's as tame as a dog! He loves to go to
town and play with kids and everybody!"

"Just the same, it's wrong to keep him in
captivity!"

Before he could think, D.J. blurted, "You're just jealous because *you* don't have him!"

They might have gotten into a real argument if the first bell hadn't rung. But as everyone started for classes, Pris asked, "Couldn't we all walk you to the post office at noon when you mail the contract?"

Everyone began to shout, "Yeah! That's a good idea!" At first, D.J. wasn't sure he wanted Pris to go along, but she hadn't done a mean thing to him since school had started in September. Except for just now, he hadn't really had an argument with Kathy either. So D.J. agreed they'd all go together.

They all got permission to leave the school grounds. At noon, they all walked with D.J. as he took the contract to the post office to buy an envelope and a stamp.

After Kathy, Pris, and Alfred touched the sealed envelope before D.J. dropped it in the slot, D.J. said, "It's just a matter of time now! I can hardly wait!"

"Me too," Alfred said, but D.J. noticed his friend didn't say it cheerfully.

D.J. slapped Alfred on the shoulder. "Hey! Maybe when they start shooting this movie, they'll let you be one of those 'extras.' "

Alfred brightened. "You think so?"

"It's worth a try," D.J. assured him. "Maybe you'll *all* get parts!"

Pris bounced up and down excitedly. Alfred grinned, but Kathy frowned. "Don't count on it! Only D.J. got a contract, and that's because he has a bear that he shouldn't be keeping!"

D.J. tried not to be annoyed with Kathy, but he really had to fight his feelings about her. She could come closer to making him upset than anybody.

One good thing came out of D.J.'s showing the cub off to different groups. It helped him get used to sharing his faith with other people. First, he had talked to his own class, then to the various school clubs, the Parent Teacher Association, and outside groups like Cub Scouts and Boy Scouts. D.J. had never planned to be a speaker, but more and more people wanted to hear about how he had helped capture Ol' Satchel Foot and Koko.

At first, D.J. mumbled and told the story with his head down. But everyone laughed and clapped so much that the boy began to get his courage up. Each time D.J. retold the story, his confidence grew.

He got the story down to where he could almost tell it in his sleep. "So while I was up in that tree, with that outlaw bear trying to get to me, I did what anybody would have: I prayed. It wasn't a big prayer, but I meant it with all my heart. I remembered what my mom had taught me about Jesus, and what I'd learned in Sunday School. So when that outlaw bear turned away, and I came down from that tree, I was a Christian. My heart had been changed, and I am different today because of what Paul Stagg calls my 'conversion experience.' "

Then D.J. went on and told about capturing Koko, and some of the adventures they'd had since then.

The one really bothersome thing in D.J.'s life that autumn was Grandpa. His cough didn't seem to get any better. He stayed in bed a lot. On good days, he sat in the old red cane-bottom rocker and read his

Bible or looked for hours across the mountains and the trees. He didn't get mad anymore and rock so hard that he went over backward. He didn't argue with Dad even when Dad got mad about something. A change had come over Grandpa. But D.J. worried about the old man getting well, especially as the months brought cold weather and the first light snowfall.

Alfred hardly seemed like the same shy, bashful stranger who had moved to Stoney Ridge last summer. Dad said it was almost like Alfred was two boys. By himself, he was still quiet and shy. But when he took Koko's lead chain, Alfred became bold. He spoke freely, his voice growing stronger. People seemed to forget his thick glasses and his skinny body and saw only a boy growing up, almost before their eyes.

Kathy said, "I've been reading about such things in Miss Kemp's class. It has to do with self-esteem. By himself, Alfred doesn't feel he's anybody. But when he's leading the bear or having him show off some of his tricks, Alfred feels he is somebody. He feels different about himself, so he acts differently. The bear brings out Alfred's hidden, inner nature."

D.J. frowned. He wasn't sure that was right, but he didn't want to argue with Kathy because they'd been getting along pretty well so far. And then Nails Abst returned to school.

"How's my bear cub?" he asked right off. "Good, I'll bet! Thanks for feeding him! I'll come by and get him some night soon."

D.J. looked at Alfred. If anything happened to Koko, the movie contract was no good. But more than that, of course, D.J. couldn't stand the idea of anything happening to the cub. The worst thing would be for Nails to take the cub. And that's the only way it would happen, D.J. decided, because he'd never give up the bear. He wouldn't do it for Kathy Stagg or anybody.

D.J. was very careful of Koko all during November and early December. Before the first snowfall, word was sent to the movie people. When they arrived and began setting up for the on-location "shoot," D.J. was ready. With Alfred, they brushed Koko until he was shining and clean as a show horse or dog. Dad drove the two boys and the cub into town that snowy Saturday morning. There D.J.'s whole world blew up!

Chapter Eleven

LIGHTS! CAMERA! ACTION!

The first day of shooting started out great for D.J. He was so excited at seeing famous movie stars walking around that he didn't mind what happened to him. He was fitted with buckskin pants and jacket and a coonskin cap for his part as an early American frontier boy. The wardrobe people took up the slack in his too-big jacket by pinning it together at the back seam. That wasn't so bad because the famous male star was having the same thing done to his fancy dress coat.

There was a disappointment for many of D.J.'s friends. The Chamber of Commerce at the county seat in Indian Springs had been flooded with requests for area people to have parts as "extras." But only a handful of people got roles, and those were all adults. The only child's part went to D.J. because of his bear. Kathy and Alfred were unable to get parts. Kathy had said it didn't really matter to

her, and Alfred honestly didn't want to be in the
movie unless he had a role with Koko. D.J. wished
Alfred had been allowed to come in with him so
they could laugh together at D.J.'s costume.

But when the makeup people began brushing
D.J.'s face with cosmetics to keep the bright lights
from reflecting off his nose and forehead, the boy
was glad none of his friends could see him.

When D.J. was ready, a young man led the
mountain boy through the old warehouse. The
wooden floor looked like a nest of snakes because
of the endless tangles of heavy electric cables that
ran in every direction. They connected to hot lights,
huge cameras on great booms,* tall sound equipment on silent wheels holding long extension micro-
phones, and all kinds of new and exciting things. The
whole set was filled with dozens of people who all
seemed to be rushing around, shouting orders.

D.J. took Koko on his chain where Alfred and
Dad had been waiting just off the set. They both
smiled and made teasing remarks about how D.J.
looked in his costume, but the young man leading
D.J. was anxious to be off. D.J. followed him
around the side of the lights and sound equipment
to where a man in cowboy clothes waited with a
big yellow bear.

"Hi," the man said, shaking D.J.'s hand and then
motioning for the big yellow bear to do the same.
"I'm Jake Zirka, and this is Atlas. But don't let the
name fool you; he's gentle, as I hope your cub is."

"Hi," D.J. replied. He looked quickly at the man
and decided he liked him. He wore blue jeans,
cowboy boots, and a black rolled-brim hat with a

rattlesnake skin band around the crown. D.J.
glanced at Koko to see how he would react to the
first other bear the cub had ever seen. Koko
reached out a forepaw and lightly tapped the 400-
pound yellow bear.

D.J. said, "They're going to be friends! Look! Your
bear's being playful too."

"That's a relief! Sometimes working with animals
can be a problem because they're still wild crea-
tures at heart, you know."

"I know," D.J. said. "I've read about the real
Grizzly Adams in history. He lived right around
here in the Sierras and had real grizzly bears for
pets. But he also trapped grizzlies, and sometimes
he got hurt bad by his bears."

"I'm glad you know about bears, D.J. Some people think Atlas is a grizzly, but he's just a plain old
California black bear in spite of his color."

"He doesn't have the humpback of a grizzly or
their color, and besides, they were much, much
bigger than black bears," D.J. said, showing off his
knowledge a little. "The last California grizzly was
seen about 1922, I think it was."

"Well, I wish we had time for more talk, but
we've got to get ready. Have you seen the script so
you know what to do?"

"SCRIPT?" D.J. exclaimed, his voice shooting up
in fright. "They told me I wouldn't have to say anything or do anything except walk someplace in this
costume with my cub beside me!"

Mr. Zirka laughed. "That's right! You're just going to do a walk-on. The director will tell you the
details, but because of the animal involved, I have

to be sure my part is done. Now, come with me
and I'll show you pretty much what you'll have to
to be sure my part is done. Now, come with me
and I'll show you pretty much what you'll have to
do when the director rolls the cameras."

It was simple, D.J. decided, when everything had
been pointed out to him. A corner of the old warehouse interior had been made to look like a log
schoolhouse. But since many frontier buildings
served more than one purpose, the schoolhouse
was also used for church meetings. D.J. would play
the part of a boy arriving at church early with his
pet bear. D.J. was to enter the room, stop and look
around, and then walk on followed by Koko. D.J.
was to sit on a backless split-log pew and open his
Bible. That was all, except he was to look up when
the male star entered in his best clothes. Then there
would be some close-up shots of the man's face
when he saw the bear. All D.J. and Koko had to do
during this was sit quietly so the sound people didn't
pick up any unwanted noise. Then the star would
order the boy and his bear out, and they would obey.

It was simple enough, so D.J. nodded his understanding and stood outside the false log school-
room-church, ready for his command. He took
slow deep breaths, trying to calm his racing heart.
He glanced around, hoping to see Dad or Alfred,
but the lights blinded him. All he could see was the
schoolroom that looked so strange because it was
open on the far side where the cameras and lights
and all the cast and crew waited.

Someone yelled, "Quiet on the set!" The noisy
preparation sounds died away. D.J. heard other

commands, but his heart was beating so fast he couldn't catch them. Then he saw the director's finger pointing at him. That was D.J.'s cue. He took a deep breath and began walking, with Koko following behind on his left without a chain or collar.

The mountain boy's heart pounded so loudly that he thought he heard the blood thumping against his ears. He walked carefully to the door, looked inside as instructed, then moved to the split-log bench and sat down. He motioned for Koko to lie down by his left foot. The bear obeyed. D.J. opened his Bible and pretended to read.

"Cut!" the director's voice made D.J. realize he'd been holding his breath. "Kid, that was great! Just great! But let's do it again, and this time, have the cub sit down by your other knee."

They did the shot over and over until D.J. began to be frustrated. He thought he was doing everything just about as perfect as possible, but after each "take," there was a suggestion and a retake. Even Koko began to be restless. He didn't want to sit down. D.J. reached down and gently pushed Koko until he sat as trained. The boy wondered what the scene must look like to Dad and Alfred who were standing somewhere behind the lights. Finally, the entire scene was done again.

Finally the director called, "That's a take! Print it!"

D.J. could hardly wait to get out from under the hot lights. The animal trainer met him, attached Koko's chain, and looked up at the boy. "It's unusual for an animal to be so calm the first time before the lights. But this little fellow seems a natural. Did you see how relaxed he was during all this shooting?"

"Koko's a city bear at heart," D.J. said proudly, removing his itchy coonskin cap and rubbing his pale blond hair. "A friend of mine keeps trying to get me to take him back to the forests and turn him loose. But I don't think he could survive in the wilderness because I've had him since he was just a few months old."

The trainer started leading the way back to the dressing room so D.J. could remove his costume and the makeup. "What're you going to do when he gets too big to handle?" he asked D.J.

The boy stopped short. "Too big to handle?"

"Sure! Now he weighs around 50 pounds, I'd guess. But in a couple of years or so, he'll top 300 pounds, maybe more. He'll scare everybody to death when you take him to town. Every dog will feel it's his duty to attack your bear. The bear will swat them too hard, and dogs will be hurt and people will be mad. No one will want him around. It'll get so bad that the animal control officer will be around often to tell you about complaints he's received. And if your bear accidentally hurts somebody, especially a child, the whole community will want your bear killed."

D.J. stood still. He'd never thought of such terrible things. "Koko wouldn't hurt anybody! Ever!"

"Not willingly, of course. But take my word for it, you've got a real tough road ahead, especially when you go off to college or the military or something and have to leave the bear behind."

The truth of Mr. Zirka's words hit the boy like a tree crashing down on him. But the terrible pain that seared through D.J.'s body was so strong he couldn't say anything. His mouth worked, but the words didn't come.

"D.J., I didn't mean to upset you, but there's absolutely no way you can keep that animal around longer than a few more months. Then what'll you do? Put him in a zoo?"

"I'd never put him behind bars like a common crook!"

"You said he wouldn't survive in the wilderness, so that's out. What's left that's fair to you and the cub?"

"I won't do *anything!*" D.J. cried wildly. "I'll keep him with me always and forever!"

The trainer slowly shook his head. "I've worked with big wild animals a long time, and I've seen what always happens. Sooner or later the animal goes back to the wild, it's given to a zoo or something like that, or it's killed."

D.J. shook his head violently. "No! That won't happen to Koko!"

But even as he spoke, D.J.'s mind leaped to something Paul Stagg had once said about the cub he'd once had years ago. Paul's bear had been less than a year old, D.J. remembered hearing, when the cub playfully swiped a kid across the face. That almost cost the child an eye. Paul had no choice but to have the cub killed or given to the zoo. Paul had chosen the zoo, but the bear wasn't happy penned up and soon died.

D.J. didn't want that to happen to Koko! The boy shook his head so hard his whole body trembled. But in that instant, D.J. suddenly knew the truth. He had been blind to the future. He had wanted the cub so much that the boy had not looked ahead to what terrible choices he faced.

The animal trainer spoke again. "I'm sorry to have upset you, D.J., but you've got to face it sooner or later. Part of growing up is the pain of responsibility. But if it's any comfort to you, I'd give that cub a good home with this production company if you want to part with him."

The boy glanced up sharply to meet Mr. Zirka's eyes. The animal trainer continued, "Why, he's such a natural ham before the cameras he might get to be a star! When you're legally old enough, you might want to come along and be my helper. Of course, we'd be gone a lot and you'd have to give up your friends and school and take private tutoring. But you'd be near your bear. That's assuming I can convince the producer to put you on the payroll. It's the only way I know that you can spend the next few years with Koko."

D.J. didn't hear any more. Somehow he managed to get out of his costume and remove the makeup. He took Koko's chain and almost stumbled back to where Dad and Alfred were waiting. They started asking him a million questions and saying what he looked like during the shooting of his scene, but D.J. wasn't listening.

*   *   *   *   *

That night, D.J. could not sleep. He lay in bed and heard the rising wind whistling outside the old frame house. He heard Koko's heavy breathing. The cub was outgrowing the small rollaway bed and had started sleeping on the floor.

D.J. tried to pray, but the pain in his heart was so great he could only moan silently with the hurt. He

tried to remember something about a Bible verse
that said the Holy Spirit prayed for somebody when
that person didn't know how to pray for himself.
But the boy couldn't remember the verse, and he
finally slipped into troubled sleep with the hope
that the animal trainer was wrong.

However, the last day before Christmas vacation
started, Dad drove the pickup into town so D.J.
could have the cub be part of an indoor Holy Land
scene. Someone had decided that since bears were
mentioned in the Bible, Koko could be in a Bethle-
hem scene with a few domestic animals. D.J.
chained Koko in the back storage room of the community clubhouse until it was time to put the cub
in the pageant. D.J. walked into the kitchen where
long tables were being loaded with all kinds of
fruitcakes, pies, cakes, fruit punch, and other refreshments. They'd be served during the intermission. The boy walked on into the small auditorium
and took a seat Alfred had saved for him.

D.J. was still wrestling with the awful thoughts
Mr. Zirka had brought up. The boy barely saw the
people who greeted each other with Christmas joy.
He didn't really hear the choir and orchestra of
towns-people who started the program.

The first community singing of a carol was interrupted by a wind storm that blew up suddenly and
rapidly increased in fury. The clubhouse soon
shook with the power of the wind. D.J. looked up
from time to time to see other people were also listening to the sounds.

He leaned over and whispered to Alfred, "You hear
that? Sounds like limbs falling on the clubhouse!"

"Sure loud and close," Alfred agreed. "But it's OK if the lights don't go out, or one of those big ever-green trees out there doesn't blow over on us."

There were more crashes and thumps, but everyone was having such a good time people ig-nored the noise and kept singing. Still, D.J. was very glad when the final carol was sung at intermission. The program chairman announced refreshments would be served in the cafeteria, then everyone was invited to see the Nativity scene with live animals. That would include D.J. Dillon's bear.

The first woman into the cafeteria let out a scream that was heard above the storm. Everyone rushed forward, squeezing in to see the reason for her screeching.

D.J. managed to get through the door. Then he stopped short. The refreshments were a total disas-ter. The refrigerator had been torn open. The huge walk-in freezer door was open and tubs of ice cream were torn with claws and the contents spread everywhere.

"That bear did it!" a woman shrieked. "Look! His tracks are everywhere—in the ice cream, the cakes, the pies, the punch—"

D.J. could almost feel the heat of the people's fury. Even though it was Christmas and they had been singing of good will among men, the sight of such utter destruction turned them into shouting, angry people.

"That bear has got to go!" a man shouted. "Somebody call the sheriff and have the animal control officer come kill that wild bear!"

D.J. was so upset he didn't recognize Alfred's

touch on his sleeve for a minute. Then the skinny boy pushed his thick glasses up on his nose and whispered, "Come on! I want to show you something!"

As people shouted and yelled about the mess, D.J. followed his friend across the messy kitchen floor and into the back storage room. Alfred pointed. "Look! Koko didn't break his chain! And there's his collar. See? It was cut!"

For a moment, D.J. didn't understand. Then it hit him. "You mean somebody deliberately turned Koko loose and opened the refrigerator and the freezer box so he could—"

"That's part of what we heard and thought was the storm. But look where the tracks go!"

D.J. saw the familiar prints, plainly visible because of the mess Koko had made and walked through. "They lead right out the door!"

"Yes, but look beside Koko's paw prints!"

D.J. bent to look. "Boot prints!"

"Exactly!" Alfred cried. "Somebody has stolen Koko!"

Chapter Twelve

A RACE AGAINST TIME

Kathy and Priscilla opened the door and peeked in. D.J. motioned for them to enter. Alfred blurted out what had happened. Kathy shook her head and exclaimed, "Oh, D.J.! Who would steal your cub?"

Pris cried, "Nails Abst! That's who!"

For a moment, D.J. considered that. "I don't know. He's always been threatening to take Koko, claiming the cub really belonged to him. But somebody was trying to buy the bear through Boot Malloy, and I don't think Nails would do that."

"Then who?" Pris demanded.

"I don't know," D.J. replied miserably.

"Could be almost anybody who's greedy," Alfred said. "Everybody's heard about the movie company's offer to buy your cub. That could mean lots of money to whoever owned Koko."

D.J. shook his head. "It wasn't a *real* offer. Mr. Zirka, the animal trainer, just talked about the possibility. But it doesn't matter now. We've got to find Koko!"

Pris cried, "In this storm?"

Alfred explained proudly, "Hero can trail Koko unless rain or snow wipes out the scent. So far, we've only got a high wind, and that won't stop Hero. But we need to get going!"

Sam Dillon stuck his head through the door from the cafeteria. "If you boys are talking about going out in this storm to look for that bear—forget it!"

D.J. protested, "Ah, Dad—!"

"It's dangerous!" Dad interrupted. "Besides, your cub'll probably be home in the morning."

"But he's been *stolen!*" D.J. exclaimed.

Paul Stagg pushed the cafeteria door open. His big body filled the frame. "What's this about your cub?" he rumbled.

D.J., Alfred, Kathy, and Pris all began explaining at once. The tall preacher held up his hands and asked D.J. to talk. The boy quickly reported what had happened. Alfred held up the cub's wide leather collar to show where it had been cut.

The two fathers nodded and talked quietly. D.J.'s dad finally spoke. "We agree there's no sense in going out in this weather. We'll have to wait for daylight."

*   *   *   *   *

The wind died at dawn. But the clouds were very flat and gray, stretching from horizon to horizon. "Snow sky," D.J. mused as he pulled a cover around him and walked to the kitchen window to look out. He turned back to the dog. "Hero, we won't have much time. Let's go wake Dad."

Dad was already pulling on his boots. "I'll make a quick breakfast for us and then we'll start looking for your bear. Better check on your grandfather first thing."

Grandpa clicked off his bedside table radio as the boy entered the front bedroom. "Just heard the weather report. Heavy snowfall expected by mid-afternoon. I hope you find your bear before then."

"Me too! You know, Grandpa, I've thought a lot about something. Whoever took Koko probably wouldn't have gone far in that windstorm. Too dangerous." D.J. sat on the edge of the bed. "How you feeling, Grandpa?"

"I've felt better, Lord knows. But I've been praying that I can lick this thing and see you graduate next spring."

The boy took the old man's brown-spotted, thin hand in both of his. "I'm counting on that. Now, Dad and I've got to start hunting for my bear. Dad's fixing breakfast for all of us. Is there anything else you need before we go?"

The old man was silent a long moment while his pale blue eyes looked steadily into his grandson's.

"What I need is something nobody except the good Lord can give: time, more time, especially when it seems to be running out. I guess a man thinks an awful lot when he's laying here in bed, weeks on end, wondering if he's going to make it."

The boy was uncomfortable with Grandpa's words, but D.J. knew that someday he would lose Grandpa even as Mom had been lost. D.J. leaned his head against the old man's whiskery face. "I love you, Grandpa," he said softly.

"I love you too."

There was a moment of wonderful warmth when neither person spoke. It was the first time either of them had ever said those words. Sometimes the boy ached to have his father say what Grandpa had just said. Finally D.J. said, "I couldn't sleep last night because my mind was doing pinwheels."

"Oh? What about?"

"For one, I've been selfish about Dad. I remember what you once said about there comes a time when a person has to let go of something, take only memories, and go forward from there."

Grandpa didn't say anything, so D.J. added, "I hope you'll understand, but I also had to give you up to the Lord. I mean. . . ." The boy stopped. He couldn't say the words.

Grandpa said them for D.J. "I understand. Sooner or later, I have to meet my Maker. But I'm hoping it's not going to be for a long while yet."

"I'm glad!" D.J. squeezed the thin hand. "It's so hard to think about it!"

"Part of growing up, D.J. Face facts like a man instead of a boy."

"I guess that's what's happening, but it hurts. I'd rather stay a boy!"

"We *all* would! But there's no stopping time."

"Guess not. Mr. Zirka, the animal trainer, made me realize I'll be going away to college in a few years. Dad'll be alone—except for you—unless I—well. . . ."

"Could you honestly let him marry the widder woman and her be your stepmother? Especially since you'd have a new stepsister who ain't never been real nice to you?"

"I'd rather not have Pris," D.J. admitted. "I'd rather not have a stepmother either. But maybe—for Dad's sake—it's time to take my memories of Mom and go on, and maybe that'll help Dad do the same."

The old man was silent a moment before he asked softly, "Have you told your father that yet?"

"Not yet."

"He'll be pleased, D.J. And he'll have a little surprise for you this morning too."

"Oh? What?"

"Guess it's OK for me to tell you, though maybe he'd like to do it hisself. You see, your dad came in here after midnight and told me he couldn't sleep either."

"I didn't hear him."

"He wanted to talk quiet-like, I guess. Anyway, he asked me if I thought he could live a Christian life."

"Really?"

"Yep. Sure surprised me."

"What'd you tell him?"

"Told him the truth: nobody can live the Christian life by hisself, but with the Holy Spirit's help, anybody can live for the Lord. So, just about the time the wind died down, your father bowed his head right where you're sitting and prayed to receive Jesus into his life!"

D.J. had a very hard time believing that, but wasn't that what Mom had said would happen someday? And hadn't everyone at church been praying for that?

Grandpa seemed to read D.J.'s mind. "You know what the Scriptures say, 'Though your sins be as scarlet, they shall be as white as snow' (Isa. 1:18, KJV). God's love does that, D.J. It covers all transgressions. Your dad's life can prove that."

* * * * *

Later, when D.J. was riding in the pickup with Dad toward Stoney Ridge, there was no sound except the truck's motor. Finally, Dad cleared his throat.

"D.J., there's something I've got to tell you."

"What's that?"

"I—well, last night, I—I was born again."

D.J. looked up at his father, bundled up against the cold in the heaterless old pickup. He said, "I'm glad! *Real* glad! That makes all three of us now, Dad! First Grandpa, then me, and now you! Mrs. Higgins will be happy too."

"I hope so."

"Dad, I've been thinking. If you want to get married again, well—I—I want you to."

Dad jerked the steering wheel and the pickup veered sharply toward the shoulder of the road. "You mean that?"

"I mean it."

For a moment, Dad drove in silence. Then he reached over and took the boy's hand. Dad's grip was so strong it almost hurt D.J. When Dad spoke, his voice nearly broke with emotion. "Thanks, Son!" he whispered.

Paul and Kathy Stagg were waiting at the community clubhouse with Alfred. Dad told the preacher about his decision for Christ, and the big man grabbed Dad in a bear hug and then thumped him on the back. Dad laughed and smiled and playfully hit Paul on the shoulder. When everyone was calmed down again, the attention turned back to the problem of finding Koko.

D.J. said, "If it was Nails who took the cub, I can't figure out how he got Koko to go with him. The bear's not too fond of Nails."

Alfred used a mittened hand to push his thick glasses up on his nose. "I've found the answer. Look."

The skinny boy bent and pointed at something shiny and red at the outside step to the community clubhouse's back door. "Strawberry jam!"

D.J. leaned closer. "Of course! Koko would follow *anybody* for some strawberry jam!"

"Well," Dad said, "let's see if your little hair-puller can pick up a trail."

Hero quickly understood he was again playing a game of hide and seek with the bear. When D.J. pushed the scruffy little dog's nose close to the back step, Hero let out a sharp bark.

"He's got a scent!" D.J. cried. "Go on, Hero! Find Koko!"

The hair-puller's short stub tail began twisting and he sniffed loudly, moving slowly away from the clubhouse. Kathy and Alfred joined D.J. in a series of excited exclamations as the dog headed for the curb. Instantly, everyone was quiet, waiting to see if the dog would lose the scent there. If he did, that meant Koko had been put into a car and driven away. There was no way any hound could trail a car.

Suddenly, Hero veered away from the curb and started up the sidewalk toward the mountains.

"Go! Hero! Go! Attaboy! Find Koko!" D.J. cried.

The little dog got into the spirit of the game. He announced his progress with loud, joyful bawls instead of his usual sharp barks. For about 20 minutes everyone followed Hero as he occasionally made a "lose," and then found the scent again. Finally, Kathy cried, "That's the end of the sidewalk, and yet he's still heading up into the mountains! There's nothing up there! Do you suppose he's making a mistake?"

Alfred sounded scornful. "Not Hero! He knows what he's doing!"

D.J. heard a car coming up fast behind them. He turned as a sheriff's patrol unit pulled up to the curb beside them. The deputy jumped out and faced the giant preacher. "Paul, I've been looking all over for you. Your wife fell down the steps and hurt herself. She's probably going to be all right, but they took her to the hospital."

In seconds, Kathy and her father were riding back down the hill toward town in the sheriff's car. Since there was nothing D.J., Dad, or Alfred could do for Mrs. Stagg, they kept up the search for Koko with Hero leading the way. The little dog was straining at his chain, his deep baying voice announcing the trail was warming up. Yet there was nothing ahead but the rising Sierra Nevada Mountains and the threatening, flat, gray snow sky.

Dad spoke. "There's no place ahead where anybody could hide a bear. Are you sure that cub isn't heading out by himself to find a den and sleep the winter away?"

The thought struck D.J. He swallowed hard and stopped to look at Alfred. The skinny kid was hunched up inside his heavy coat. His nose was red and his glasses were partly steamed up from breathing into the icy mountain air. But Alfred shook his head.

"Remember, we're all pretty sure we've seen boot tracks a couple of times."

Dad removed his stocking cap and scratched his head. "Just the same, I'd better go back and get the pickup. It's going to be a long walk back, and if that dog doesn't find the cub pretty soon, it'll be too late because the snowstorm's going to break any time!"

In a few minutes, Dad was out of sight. D.J. glanced at the heavy, dark sky which seemed ready to burst with snow. Suddenly, Hero threw up his head and bawled loudly. D.J. exclaimed, "He's winded the cub!"

The scruffy little hair-puller made a sharp right turn and dashed away from the roadway, pulling hard at the chain. The baying was steady and excited, leading up to the 'treed' sound. D.J. exclaimed, "Hero's got him 'lined out'! In a minute, Hero'll be 'looking at him'!"

Alfred stumbled and almost fell because his hands were thrust deep into his coat pockets. "D.J., there's nothing over there but the school!"

"Exactly! And because it's Christmas vacation, nobody's there!"

"Except whoever stole Koko?"

"Right! Come on! Let's go!"

The trail led across the school yard, around in back of the auditorium, and past the buildings to the bus sheds. Hero's baying was steady now; one fast chopping bawl after another. He ran to the side metal door and leaped upon it, his nails scratching frantically on the slick metal.

"We've found him!" Alfred exclaimed. "Hero's found Koko!"

D.J. dropped the dog's chain and tried the door handle. "It's locked! But at least we've found my cub!"

A voice behind them said, "No, you didn't! All you've found is *trouble!*"

D.J. and Alfred spun around. Hero growled, his hackles* rising and his upper lip curling back from his fangs.

"Nails!" D.J. cried. "You stole my bear!"

"*My* bear, you mean!" The older boy thumped a short, curved crowbar in his gloved left hand. "Make your mutt back off or I'll give him a headache!"

D.J. reached down and patted Hero. "It's OK! Quiet! Quiet! That's a good dog."

Alfred asked, "Where's Koko?"

"Inside, sleeping off all that junk he ate last night."

D.J. snuggled Hero close to his left leg and faced the older boy. "*Sleeping?* At this time of day? You sure he's not sick?"

D.J. saw a flicker of emotion cross the older boy's face. Nails licked his lips. "Well, he has been sorta quiet since last night."

"Let me see him!" D.J. demanded.

The cub was curled up in a large metal oil drum that had been tipped on its side. It smelled as if it had once held sawdust for sweeping the oil drippings off the bus shed floor. Hero dashed into the drum and began playfully growling and biting the cub. The bear did not move. D.J. dropped to his knees, pulled the dog out of the barrel, and felt the bear. The cub still did not move.

Alfred cried, "He's dead! Nails, you've killed Koko!"

Chapter Thirteen

A NEW HOME FOR KOKO

D.J. examined Koko for a long moment, feeling and talking to him. Slowly, D.J. stood up and said, "His heart's still beating, but very, very slowly."

Alfred exclaimed, "We've got to get him to the vet!"

D.J. shook his head. "No! Nails wanted Koko enough to steal him. Let him take Koko to the vet."

Alfred yelled, "D.J.! Are you nuts?"

D.J. frowned. "How about it, Nails?"

The older boy hesitated. "I don't want no bear that's dying!"

D.J. persisted, "You always said Koko was rightfully yours! Isn't that right?"

"Sure! I knew sooner or later I'd get him! My dad kept trying to buy the cub through Boot Malloy, but when you were so stubborn—"

D.J. interrupted, "You stole him! You take care of him!"

Nails backed up, lifting the crowbar. "Now hold

on a minute! I want that cub to sell to the movie people! But he's no good dead!"

D.J. pointed to the cub which hadn't stirred. "I'll give you a paper right now that says I'm giving up all rights to the bear."

"No, you don't!" Nails yelled.

Alfred pulled frantically on D.J.'s coat sleeve, but D.J. didn't seem to notice.

Nails shook his head hard. "I don't want no dead bear!"

D.J. shrugged. "Well, suppose he recovers?"

Nails frowned, then quickly bent and stuck his hand into the barrel. While Nails' head was turned away, D.J. looked hard at Alfred. D.J. shook his head very hard but briefly. Alfred blinked, not understanding, but before he could say anything, Nails turned to watch D.J. and Alfred. Nails' right hand was deep inside the barrel. It was obvious he was feeling the bear's heartbeat. He stood up. "It's almost stopped. He's your bear — take him!"

D.J. shook his head. "Not unless you give me a paper saying you don't have any claim to Koko."

Alfred had almost begun crying. But when Nails said, "OK! OK! Give me a piece of paper," the skinny kid reached into his pocket and brought out a notepad and pencil stub.

D.J. told Nails, "Write this down: 'I hereby give up any claim to the bear cub called Koko.' "

Nails wrote slowly, his tongue working over his lips until it was done. D.J. told him to sign and date it, which Nails did.

D.J. took the paper, glanced at it, and then tucked it inside his heavy coat pocket. "OK, Alfred, let's find some way to carry Koko. And Nails, I hope you never steal anything else, because in the long run, you're going to lose!"

Suddenly, something that had been bothering D.J. for months was easy to do. "Nails, I know you never go to church and I don't suppose you think much about the Lord. But I want you to know I believe in Him, and I'm trying hard to live like it. If you ever want to talk about such things, let me know."

Nails didn't say anything for a minute. "Believe what you want," he said finally and turned to look out the window.

D.J. took off his heavy coat and laid it on the concrete floor in front of the barrel. Alfred knelt beside him, whispering under his breath, but D.J. gave him a warning glance to keep quiet. Slowly, carefully, the friends worked the bear cub onto the coat. Koko barely moved. He made a little growling sound, but that was all. Then D.J. and Alfred lifted the coat with the bear in it. They carried their burden out the door. It had started to snow lightly.

Sam Dillon saw them from the roadway and drove the pickup straight to them. He jumped out and called, "You found him! Is he dead?"

D.J. looked back at Nails, who had been standing in the falling snow outside the bus shed. The older boy turned and started running across the school yard toward the mountains.

Alfred answered Dad. "Not yet! But he's dying! Quick! Let's get him to the vet!"

D.J. helped Dad lift the cub gently into the back end of the pickup. "There's no hurry, Alfred."

"No hurry? D.J., you're crazy!"

Dad carefully checked the cub, covered him with the coat, and then turned to grin at the boys. "D.J.'s right, Alfred. There's no hurry."

Alfred's face showed mixed pain and surprise at the difference between the words and Dad's grin. But D.J. was also smiling. Alfred yelled, "What's going on?"

Patting Alfred's shoulder, D.J. said, "Koko's starting to sleep for the winter!"

Snow was settling on Alfred's glasses, frosting the lenses. He slapped his mittened hand to his forehead. "Of course! Hibernation! I got so scared thinking Koko was dying that I didn't think of that!"

"Neither did Nails," D.J. said.

* * * * *

A few weeks later, Mrs. Stagg was almost fully recovered from her fall down the steps, except she had to hobble around on crutches. Grandpa was well enough that on nice days he walked with the help of his Irish shillelagh and sat in his rocker on the front porch.

After a lot of thinking, D.J. had changed his selfish feelings about wanting to keep Koko. He finally realized what was best for the bear. He would give Koko to Mr. Zirka, the animal trainer.

Still, D.J. hurt inside when it came time to say good-bye to Koko for the last time. The weather had warmed up a little that day. As bears do sometimes, Koko came out of hibernation for a while. Dad, Alfred, Kathy, and Pris stood with D.J. when he petted the cub and turned Koko over to the gentle animal trainer. There were some tears, but finally the friends all walked away, trying not to feel too terrible.

D.J. struggled to keep his voice steady as he said

again, "It's best for Koko. And I'll always have my memories."

"We'll all have our memories of that little cub," Kathy added.

Pris sniffed. "I'll never forget Koko!"

"Neither will I," Alfred added. He adjusted his thick glasses and smiled. "Besides, we can have other adventures."

Dad cleared his throat. "How about starting with the new family we're going to have when Hannah Higgins and Priscilla take the Dillon name? Paul Stagg's going to perform the ceremony in church at Easter. Would all of you kids like to take part in the wedding?"

There was a chorus of happy agreement. Only Alfred looked a little disappointed. D.J. asked, "What's the matter?"

Alfred said, "I wasn't talking about that kind of adventure! I meant something like having another exciting pet or solving a mystery."

D.J. laughed and slapped his friend on the shoulder. "I don't have any doubt that'll happen, Alfred! No doubt at all!"

* * * * *

The next adventure would soon start on the roadway not far from where they stood. There a frightened puppy would crouch on the double yellow lines of the mountain highway while cars whizzed by in both directions. Read about it in the next episode of the D.J. Dillon Adventure Series:

Dooger, The Grasshopper Hound.

LIFE IN STONEY RIDGE

ANTIBIOTICS: Any of a group of chemical substances, including penicillin, used to treat infectious diseases.

BOOMS: Beams on a mobile crane used to hold or move a movie camera or a microphone.

CHOKE-SETTER: A lumberman who prepares downed trees for the heavy equipment that will take the trees out of the woods. The choke-setter digs a hole or tunnel under the downed tree trunk. Then he throws a strong steel cable over the log and pulls it back through the hole. He puts the knob on one end of the cable through a loop on the other end and pulls the cable tight around the log. A tread-type tractor then hooks onto the log and pulls it out of the woods.

CONIFERS: Another name for the many cone-bearing evergreen trees or shrubs. Spruce, fir, and pine trees are all conifers.

CRACKLINGS: A dog food made of pork scraps or trimmings that have been heated and pressed to get rid of most of the fat.

GREEN CHAIN: As freshly cut trees are sawed and turned into boards at the lumber mill, the boards fall onto a chain conveyer belt. This belt carries the green, heavy boards to be stacked before going into the kiln for drying.

HACKLES: The hair on a dog's neck and back that stands up when the dog is angry or afraid.

HAIR-PULLING BEAR DOG: A small, quick dog of mixed breed. A hair-puller's natural tendency is to go for the heels or backside of any animal, including sheep, cows, or bears. This mutt is also called a "heeler" or "cut-across" dog.

IRISH SHILLELAGH (pronounced "Shuh-**LAY**-Lee"): A cudgel or short, thick stick often used for a walking cane. A shillelagh is usually made of blackthorn saplings or oak and is named after the Irish village of Shillelagh.

OMNIVOROUS: An animal that will eat anything, including other animals and plant food.

OXBLOOD: A dull, deep red color.

PONDEROSA TREE: A large North American tree used for lumber. Ponderosa pines usually grow in the mountain regions of the west and can reach heights of 200 feet. The ponderosa pine is the state tree of Montana.

PROPRIETOR: The owner of a business or store.

SET-TO: Another way of referring to a strong, private conversation.

SUGAR PINE: The largest of the pine trees. A sugar pine can grow as tall as 240 feet. Its cones range from 10 to 26 inches long and are often used for decoration.

TAMP: To pack in tightly by lightly tapping with repeated strokes.

VINDICTIVE NATURE: A spiteful or vengeful attitude. A vindictive person likes to get even with people who mistreat him.

WINDED: A bear hunter's expression that means that the dog has gotten close enough to smell the bear's scent in the air or on the wind and not just on the trail the bear had left.

D.J. Dillon
· ADVENTURE SERIES ·

The Hair-Pulling Bear Dog
D.J.'s ugly mutt gets a chance to prove his courage.

The Bear Cub Disaster
When his pet bear causes trouble in Stoney Ridge, D.J. realizes he can't keep the cub forever.

Dooger, The Grasshopper Hound
D.J. and his buddy Alfred rely on an untrained hound to save Alfred's little brother from a forest fire.

The Ghost Dog of Stoney Ridge
D.J. and Alfred find out what's polluting the mountain lakes — and end up solving the ghost dog mystery.

Mad Dog of Lobo Mountain
D.J. struggles to save his dog's life and learns a hard lesson about responsibility.

The Legend of the White Raccoon
Is the white raccoon real or only a phantom? As D.J. tries to find out, he stumbles upon a dangerous secret.

The Mystery of the Black Hole Mine
D.J. battles "gold" fever, and learns an eye-opening lesson about his own selfishness and greed.

Ghost of the Moaning Mansion
Will D.J. and Alfred get scared away from the moaning mansion before they find the "real" ghost?

The Secret of Mad River
D.J.'s dog is an innocent victim — and so is the hermit of Mad River. Can D.J. prove the hermit's innocence before it's too late?

Escape Down the Raging Rapids
D.J.'s life depends on reaching a doctor soon, but forest fires and the dangerous raging rapids of Mad River stand in his way.

*Look for these exciting stories
at your local Christian bookstore.*